LOVE BY THE BOOK

Kevin kissed me lightly, and his lips felt warm and gentle. "You're so sweet, Lisa," he murmured. He was about to kiss me again when a car pulled up. I pulled away reluctantly.

Phil came bouncing up the steps. "I got some great antiques and terrific children's books at that auction!" he said enthusiastically.

Kevin broke in. "Phil's working with you, Lisa?" He didn't sound pleased.

Phil glanced at him for the first time, and his smile faded. "I'm her new assistant," he explained.

Kevin looked uncomfortable, and I could tell he disapproved. *Wow!* I thought. *Kevin's really jealous.* Noticing how Phil's enthusiasm had faded, I felt a little guilty. But I could never be romantically interested in him. And now I knew the boy I had dreamed of for months really cared about me.

Bantam Sweet Dreams Romances
Ask your bookseller for the books you have missed

Love by the Book

Anne Park

BANTAM BOOKS

TORONTO · NEW YORK · LONDON · SYDNEY · AUCKLAND

RL 6, IL age 11 and up

LOVE BY THE BOOK
A Bantam Book / April 1985

Sweet Dreams and its associated logo are registered trademarks of Bantam Books, Inc. Registered in U.S. Patent and Trademark Office and elsewhere.

Cover photo by Pat Hill.

ISBN 0-553-24823-5

Published simultaneously in the United States and Canada

PRINTED IN THE UNITED STATES OF AMERICA

O   0 9 8 7 6 5 4 3 2 1

*This book is for
Tina and Chris*

Chapter One

The heavily waxed, slanted wood floors of Randall's Bookstore and Antique Shop shone in the early-June sunshine. Even our store's shabbiness was made beautiful by the sun. *I love this place*, I thought. *I love every single old book and antique in it.* Hugging a tattered copy of *Harriet the Spy* to my chest, I had to laugh at myself. I really hated the idea of having some stranger buy the book because I had adored it so much when I was a little girl. But how many copies of a favorite childhood book did one person need? *One, Lisa Randall*, I told myself firmly. *And you already have two at home.*

I added *Harriet* to a stack of other old

books and took them out front to the long, narrow porch that ran the length of the building. The plain wooden table was already full of dusty volumes, so I spread the new stack out on the old-fashioned school desk. Then I dusted the whole display.

I guess books are in the Randall blood. My grandfather started this shop with my grandmother and my father helping out. Then, when my grandparents moved to Florida, my mother and father took over the shop. I've helped, too, ever since I was old enough to shelve the books.

The trouble was, the shop wasn't making enough money to support us anymore. My father had to take a job in Rochester, New York, and my mother was working, too, at a part-time job. The shop was up for sale, and if my father found a buyer for it, a whole chunk of my life would be gone. *Maybe no one will want to buy it,* I thought. But I knew that wasn't likely. It was such a delightful little place.

I looked around the store slowly. It did look appealing. Someone would like it. The tourists sure did. They always stopped to browse, and sometimes to buy, as they passed through our little town. Then again, we were just about the only attraction in Kingsway.

But that didn't matter. I loved it here.

Kingsway was the perfect place for me. Sometimes I think I was born in the wrong century. This tiny village with its tree-lined side streets and gingerbread houses belonged to the nineteenth century more than the twentieth. I knew every single person there and that made me feel confident. At school in Bragdon, about ten miles away, I wasn't so sure of myself. There were four hundred students there, lots of them strangers from surrounding towns, and I felt a little shy and self-conscious with them.

Kevin Cott was one of that four hundred, and I thought he was the most perfect boy in the whole school—even in the entire world. He had dark, wavy hair and brown eyes that made you want to melt. His family had lived in many different parts of the world because his father's business took him to foreign countries. I guess that's one reason all the girls in school were crazy about Kevin. He was so sophisticated and sure of himself. The Central High boys seemed like small-town hicks beside him, even the ones who ran with his crowd—his and Meredith Hunt's.

I was arranging another stack of books on the porch when a boy's voice said, "Hi, Lisa."

I looked up hopefully, but the face wasn't the one I'd been wishing for. It was only Phil Bradley.

"Hi, Phil. How're things?"

"Fine. Need some help?" Without waiting for an answer, he jumped over the railing and onto the low porch and grabbed the feather duster from me. He raised such a cloud of dust that I started to sneeze.

"You're supposed to get rid of the dust with that thing," I gasped. "Not stir up a storm!"

He laughed and began to work with less gusto while I went inside for more books.

It was nine o'clock on Saturday morning, and the traffic would be streaming through town soon. People who went through Kingsway were on their way to larger places, of course, but at least they kept things lively—although not so lively as they'd been before the new expressway diverted some of the traffic. Fewer people passed through Kingsway now, and that was why the bookstore wasn't making so much money.

I sighed and picked up another load of books. Getting upset wasn't going to help the store do any better. I shouldered my way through the door and onto the porch, my arms full of books. I found my helper sitting on the porch railing, looking at a book. I studied him for a minute, before he even realized I was there. Phil Bradley was tall and lanky, with hair just about the color of the sun on a

4

hot August morning, and a nice, lopsided smile. I knew he liked me, but when I compared him to Kevin Cott, with his dark hair and his brown eyes, I knew Phil couldn't ever be what I wanted.

He looked up then, his blue eyes barely focusing on me. He had that look serious readers get when they have to bring themselves back to this world from their book worlds.

"I'd almost forgotten about the Hardy boys," he said. "My uncle gave me his whole collection when I was about ten, and I was a Hardy boys freak for a while. My mother gave them away when we left Brooklyn Heights. I want to buy this one, just for old times' sake."

I swept a bow at him. "Be my guest," I said. "My dad's always giving away books to people who especially love them. Consider that a gift."

He didn't protest, the way some people would. He seemed to know it made me feel good to give him a little gift. He thanked me and laid the book on his jacket, which he'd tossed on the little antique plant stand in a corner of the porch.

He went on dusting books and arranging them in neat stacks by author—something my father never had time to do anymore.

"It still feels funny," Phil said, staring out at the lack of traffic on our main street.

"What does?"

"Being in Kingsway instead of Brooklyn Heights."

"Which do you like better?" I asked him curiously.

"Well, I guess I miss the noise and the people of the city, but I kind of like it here. It's fantastic to see trees and flowers." He grinned. "And the other day, when I was out hiking, I ran into a cow! You don't get any of those in Brooklyn!"

I laughed. "I've known them all my life."

He looked straight at me. "I wish I'd known *you* all my life, Lisa."

I couldn't think of anything to say except, "Thank you."

Phil had moved to our tiny village from New York City about six months earlier. His parents had decided they were tired of the Big Apple rat race, and just like that, they'd bought a large, sunny-yellow home on one of the hilly side streets. The year before, Mr. and Mrs. Bradley and Phil and his little brother, Joey, had driven through Kingsway on their way to Canada, and they'd decided this was the place for them. Apparently, Mr. Bradley didn't object to the rat race in Rochester because every day he drove there to his job with one of the big manufacturing companies.

"How about something to drink?" Phil asked, breaking into my thoughts.

"Oh, sure," I said. "We have tea or coffee or soda."

"Tea would be great," he said.

We went into the shop, which used to be an old farmhouse years and years ago. The floors were made of wide, soft pine and the wall between the former dining and living rooms had been knocked down, so there was one long room, lined with bookshelves.

The antiques were placed in strategic spots around the room. A butter churn was in one corner, an old spinning wheel in another. We had a wood-burning stove and old-fashioned display cases containing jewelry and silver spoons, Spanish combs and ivory fans. I guess none of the stuff was terribly valuable, but I loved all the old things. It was like living in a fairytale.

"Lisa," Phil said patiently, "you have that look again! I can always tell when you're dreaming because your eyes get kind of foggy and you stand perfectly still."

"It takes one to know one," I said, and we headed toward the kitchen together, laughing.

I lit a match under a gas jet and put the kettle on. I decided to make tea in a teapot, using loose tea, because it seemed to fit in with my mood.

Because my family spent so much time at the store, there were always snacks in the kitchen. That day there were English muffins and homemade jam, and even though Phil said he'd had breakfast before he left, he put away three muffins.

"Good stuff," he said, his mouth full. "And great tea." He took a sip.

Sometimes I wondered why Phil hung around me. Unlike me, he'd fitted right in at Central High, almost from the day he'd enrolled there. He had an easy way about him that other kids liked. Maybe it was because he came from a big city. He wasn't tough or anything, just comfortable talking to people.

My best friend, Kimberly, thought he was great. "He's cute, Lisa. I almost wish I weren't going out with Steve. I'd go after him! But I know he likes you. Can't you be a little nicer to him?" she had said to me a few days earlier.

I had replied haughtily, "I'm not in the least interested in Phil Bradley, except as a friend, so save your sales talk. You know there's only one boy in the whole school that I'd want to go out with. Kevin Cott."

Which shows you the kind of dreamer I was, because I knew I was just as likely to have a date with Tom Cruise or Matt Dillon as I was with Kevin Cott.

Kimberly was blunt. "I know you like him,

Lisa, but he's taken. Meredith Hunt isn't going to hand Kevin over to you." She was too polite to add that Kevin had never shown any desire to be handed over.

Wistfully I thought that it would be fun to have a steady boyfriend, to be able to plan on going to parties and movies without wondering who would take me. Oh, I dated some, but it wasn't the same as having someone special.

"What are you thinking about now, dreamer?" Phil asked curiously.

I could feel myself blushing, but I said, "Nothing, just off in a trance instead of working. I should be out there, watching for customers."

Phil took our cups over to the sink. "Speaking of which, have you talked to your dad about his letting you take over the place?"

"Uh, not yet," I admitted. Phil had this wild idea that I could run the shop by myself. Well, maybe it wasn't that wild. It *would* be one way to keep it in our family, but I didn't know if I was ready to handle the responsibility.

In any event, we didn't have time to discuss it further, for I heard a car pull up to the store.

Phil started washing the dishes, and I went out on the porch to greet our customer. I gasped when I recognized the boy at the wheel of the blue Sentra. Kevin Cott! Quickly I ran back into the store and glanced in the antique mirror, which hung just inside the door. Tousled, dark-blond hair, blue eyes, a smear of strawberry jam at one corner of my mouth. Mentally, in that brief moment, I compared myself with Meredith Hunt, who had long, dark brown, wavy hair, a perfect complexion and a beautifully proportioned figure. Just thinking about her made me feel too tall—I'm five-eight—and too thin.

Kevin was just coming up the steps as I made my way back onto the porch. "Hi, Lisa." Those were the same words Phil had used, but spoken in Kevin's sexy voice, they seemed entirely different and weighted with meaning.

My heart turned over. But I managed to say, "Hello, Kevin. You're out bright and early."

"Well, early at least."

I laughed, and he gave me an approving look, as though he was pleased because I'd acknowledged his little joke. I was hoping he'd just dropped by, but he said, "I'm looking for a birthday present for my mother, and she's crazy about antiques. I thought you might be able to suggest something."

"Come on inside."

I led him to a case of small items: combs, spoons, perfume flasks, cameo brooches, and

Victorian hat pins. Kevin poured over everything carefully for a while, then asked me to take out a glass perfume bottle with an intricate network of silver filigree.

"I think she'll love this."

"Would you like me to gift wrap it for you?"

"Sure. Thanks."

He leaned up against one of the wooden showcases. "Are you going to be working here all summer?"

He was making conversation with *me.* "I guess so," I told him. "*If* we're still here. My father is thinking of selling the place."

"Hey, he can't do that! Randall's Bookstore has been in Kingsway ever since I can remember."

All of a sudden I could hardly hold back the tears. I couldn't bear the thought of someone taking down that weather-beaten wooden sign and putting up a new one with a strange name on it.

Kevin was looking at me for an explanation, and I said, "My father just took a job in Rochester because the expressway has cut down on the traffic through Kingsway and he can't make ends meet. I suppose my mother and I will keep the store running until we sell it, but she's working, too, so she doesn't have that much time."

"That's rough," he said.

I put the perfume bottle in tissue, then in a nice white box, and began to wrap it in beautiful blue paper with little white birds flying across it. We continued talking. It was easy! I really didn't feel shy with Kevin. There were just so many things I wanted to ask him.

"I heard you lived in London for a year," I said. "What was it like? Did you go to Harrod's and Abbey Lane and the Old Curiosity Shop?"

He looked surprised. "Have you been there?"

I shook my head. "Only in books and movies. But I *plan* to go there someday. I've always wanted to ride on an English train. Did you?"

"As a matter of fact, I did." And he started telling me about England, things I'd always wanted to know. It was like taking a trip there myself, and I could tell he enjoyed describing it to me. "You should go there, Lisa," he said seriously.

"Someday I will." I felt as though I were making him a solemn promise.

He was looking at me as though he were seeing me for the first time, not just as a tall, shy girl who happened to go to the same school he did, but as a real person, an interesting person. "You're different, Lisa. You have lots more imagination than most girls," Kevin said.

At that moment Phil appeared from the kitchen. I'd absolutely forgotten about him.

Kevin and Phil greeted each other, and we all talked about school for a little while. They both were basketball fanatics, so they had that in common. But Phil didn't belong in Kevin's "in" crowd any more than I did.

Finally Kevin said he had to go, but he seemed reluctant. "Well, see you at school Monday." He was looking straight at me, as though he weren't including Phil in that statement.

"I hope your mother likes the perfume bottle," I said.

He smiled, that gorgeous, melting smile of his. "Thanks for helping me choose it and for doing such a great job of wrapping it. And try to talk your father out of selling Kingsway's landmark."

I walked out on the porch with him and waved him on his way. Then I went back inside. Phil was standing there, looking glum. I had the feeling he didn't like Kevin much.

But it wasn't Kevin he wanted to talk about. "I don't know what you're waiting for, Lisa. The time to talk to your folks is now. There are only a couple more weeks of school left, then you could take over for the summer full-time and on weekends in the fall. You've grown up in this business, so you know how to handle it."

"I don't know," I said. "I've never had full responsibility for the store. And since Mom and Dad are both working, I wouldn't be able to count on them to help out much."

"You wouldn't have to," Phil said. "You know the inventory, right?" I nodded my head. "And the pricing system?" I nodded again. "And how to shop at sales? And scout out antiques? And wait on customers?"

"Yes, but I don't know when I'd shop for more inventory, and I don't know how to keep the books."

"You could count on me for those things." He was smiling, but I knew he was serious.

"You really think I can make a go of this on my own?"

"It doesn't really matter if I do, if you don't," Phil noted.

"You know, it might work out," I said, starting to smile. "I'd have to work out the hours, of course, after school starts again. Maybe keep it open from three-thirty to six on some weekdays and all day Saturday and Sunday."

"And maybe your mom could stay here a couple of afternoons a week when she's not working," he offered.

My mind was reeling with the possibili-

14

ties. "I'll ask my dad tonight. Oh, he's got to let me try—"

"What can he lose, except maybe his shirt?" Phil quipped. "Anyway, you have nothing to lose for asking."

"If he lets me do it, I'm going to need some help. How would you like a summer job, Phil? It wouldn't pay much, but you'd get a chance to read all these books."

"Throw in a few English muffins and you're on." He grinned. "I'll call you tonight and see what the good word is."

"OK."

He practically danced down the porch steps as he waved goodbye. I was really excited about the idea of keeping the shop going. But deep down, somewhere beneath the enthusiasm, I felt disappointed. The wrong boy had said, "I'll call you tonight."

Chapter Two

"The meal looks yummy," I told my mother as I sat at the dinner table that evening. The table was pretty, too, with a large glass platter of antipasto in the center, tall glasses of iced tea on the blue woven placemats, and a plate of fluffy rolls.

I liked our dining room. The floors were wood, which my father had refinished himself, and the walls were covered with a small print blue-and-white wallpaper. The table was an antique pine trestle, also restored by my dad. A bay window looked out into the side yard, where a tangle of garden flowers brightened up the room in the spring and summer. The dining room was old-fashioned, like our whole house, but it was also warm and cozy. I thought it fitted the Randalls.

Still, I had a feeling it wasn't going to be too easy to talk them into letting me run the shop. I knew we needed the money from the sale, for one thing. Mom had had pneumonia the previous year, and the bills had mounted up. And sixteen-year-old girls don't often become managers of stores. I decided to wait until after we'd eaten to bring up Phil's idea. Everyone would probably be relaxed and easier to talk to then.

During the meal Mom and Dad told me what they'd bought in the city that day—two lawn chairs and some T-shirts for Mom and me.

"How were things at the shop?" Dad asked.

"Not bad." I tried not to smile too broadly. "Kevin Cott came by and bought a perfume bottle for his mother's birthday."

Mom raised her eyebrows. "Humph, I'd expect him to go to the most expensive jewelry store in Rochester."

"Mom! You make him sound like a snob, and he's not. He's very nice."

I could see her looking at me a little curiously. "Sorry. That wasn't fair of me. I'm afraid I'm judging him by his mother." Then she laughed. "That's terrible, isn't it? Just

18

reverse snobbery on my part. Don't pay any attention to me, Lisa. If we had lots of money, I'd probably throw it around like crazy, too."

"I wouldn't," Dad said thoughtfully. "I'd buy a few rare books, just for myself—not to sell—and perhaps an expensive accordion." My father was the only person I knew who loved to play the accordian.

"Books and an accordion." Mom smiled at my father. "Of course, that's what you'd want, Smitty. And you deserve to get them, too. Perhaps when you sell the shop."

That gave me the chance I'd been waiting for. But just as I began to open my mouth, Dad put his hands on the table and coughed to indicate he had an announcement to make. "The shop, yes, I was getting to that," he said. "I've been doing a lot of thinking. This new job of mine's been eating up most of my time. And with costs being what they are, I don't see how we can keep running the shop. I'd hoped to wait till we got a buyer, but I think we're going to have to close it up now."

"You can't do that!" I could hear my voice cracking with emotion. This wasn't the calm, businesslike way I'd wanted to approach the subject, but I couldn't help it. I rushed on, the words coming out in a tumble. "Please, Dad, you can't close now. I could try to keep it going."

"I'd love it if you could, but you're in school, honey."

"But Mom and I are managing it all right now, and when school's out I'll be able to work full-time. And I need a job, Dad. Where else in Kingsway am I going to find one?"

"She has a point there," Mom interjected. It was clear where her sympathies lay.

I continued. "And Phil Bradley said he'd help. He loves books, too. And I'm sure we could manage between us. Couldn't I please try?"

My father said slowly, "The shop hasn't been bringing in much money. We're still going to have to sell it."

"I know," I said, though in my heart I hoped he'd change his mind about that. "But I can run it until then. I know I can. Besides, a working store's going to be more appealing to a buyer than a shuttered-up old building."

"That's true," he admitted.

Mom was watching both of us. "I wonder, Smitty," she said, smiling at me. "Granted, Lisa is pretty absentminded when her nose is stuck in a book, but she's a good salesperson. Maybe we should give her a chance. What do you think?"

Dad's face slowly broke into a grin, and he winked at me. "Give us a little time to talk, hon, and we'll let you know."

I jumped to my feet. "I'll get the dessert, then I have to call Kimberly."

"Nothing's settled," my father warned.

"I know. But I have to tell her about the *possibility*!" My parents both laughed, and I went to serve the brownies.

The ivory push-button phone was one of the few modern things in my room, and I liked it because I paid for it myself with my earnings from the store. I punched in Kimberly's number, and she answered right away. Since she has two older brothers and a sister, she has to grab her turn at the telephone.

"I was just going to call you," she said, "before Bonnie gets the phone. Steve's coming over after a while, and it's no fun talking while he's here. How can I talk about him when he's right in the room?"

Kimberly and Steve had been dating each other since they were fourteen, and they made a really great couple. I towered over both of them. Kimberly was short and cute, with silky but short black hair and brown eyes. Steve wasn't very tall, either, and his hair was reddish-brown and curly. I'd known them since the day I was born, practically, and I felt really comfortable with them.

After we'd gone through the preliminary "What's new?" and "How're things?" I told

Kimberly about Phil's idea for keeping the bookshop going.

"Do you think your parents will go for it?"

"They're in conference right now. I'm hoping." Then I couldn't restrain myself any longer. "Guess who came into the store this morning to buy his mother a birthday gift?"

"Not Kevin?"

I knew I sounded hysterically happy, but I couldn't help it. "You bet!"

"You're kidding!"

"In the flesh, the beautiful flesh." After that, I described in minute detail every second of Kevin's visit, how he looked, what he said, what he was wearing. Kimberly was an excellent listener. "Then Phil came in from the kitchen, and, Kimberly, I'd forgotten he was there!"

"Poor Phil," she said, and I could tell from her tone she really meant it.

"I know, I felt guilty. Actually, it was Phil's idea to keep the store running. If my father goes for it, I'm giving him a part-time job at Randall's. That's settled already."

"He *likes* you, Lisa. And you'll be thrown together every day if he works for you. Maybe something will come of it."

I sighed. "Nothing will come of it. Phil is a friend, that's all. I couldn't possibly fall in love with him." *Because I love someone truly won-*

derful, I added silently. I knew Kimberly thought I was out of my mind to fall in love with Kevin. He was out of my league. And he was already seeing Meredith Hunt.

"Soon after I hung up with Kimberly, the phone rang. It was Phil. "What did your folks say?" he asked.

"The situation's even worse than I thought. Dad was thinking of closing up completely, though I may have talked him out of it. He's talking it over with Mom."

"While they're thinking, how would you like to go up to Polly's for some ice cream? My mom said I could take the car."

"Sure, I'd like that. Be ready in fifteen minutes."

My mother and father beamed when I told them Phil was picking me up. I knew they liked him, partly because of his easygoing personality and partly because he was a book lover. And when my father found out that Phil liked to play chess, I think he was ready to adopt him.

"Your mother and I have been talking," Dad said when I went downstairs to find Phil already there. "And we've decided, since you've been helping out at the shop for quite a while now, that you must know the business well enough to give it a try."

23

"Mom! Dad!" I shrieked happily. I gave them each a rib-breaking hug.

"It won't be easy," my father warned me. "And this is just an experiment. If you go in the red, we'll have to close up. It will be a lot of work. In addition to running the store, you'll have to keep records and get to auctions and garage sales to acquire new stock."

"I can take her, Mr. Randall," Phil said eagerly. "I'm sure my mother will let me take her car when we need it." He stopped then, blushing a little. "That is, if you mean to hire me."

Dad gave a little chuckle. "From now on, Lisa does the hiring and firing, but I gather she intends to hire you."

I stuck out my hand to Phil. "You've got yourself a job. The pay won't be great, but if we build up the business, I might give you a raise!"

"We'll discuss the details later," Dad said. "Right now, I think I'll play the accordion for a while. Enjoy your drive."

Mom gave me a kiss and said, "Congratulations on your new partnership, you two."

As my parents turned back toward the living room, Phil and I left. Outside in the light of the June moon, Phil and I smiled at each other, elated. I almost hugged him, but decided that wouldn't be such a great idea.

"This is going to be a good summer, Lisa," he said as he opened the car door for me. "You are now the proprietor of a book and antique shop, and you already have one employee! What other sixteen-year-old girl can say that?"

Chapter Three

Bragdon was a little larger than Kingsway, but it was just a pinpoint on the map, even so. It didn't have a movie theater or a library, but it did have a big supermarket and a few stores and restaurants in addition to the high school. Polly's Sweet Shoppe was the most popular place to go for miles around. It looked like the malt shop in "Happy Days" or in an old movie. There were a few tables and lots of wooden booths and a tile floor and ceiling fans. The burgers and ice cream were so good that people came from every little town around just to snack there.

"Hi, Lisa, hi, Phil. Come on over!" It was Kimberly and Steve, sitting at a round table in the center of the room. I knew they'd have preferred a secluded booth, but Polly's was crowded. We went over and joined them.

"What'll you have, boss?" Phil asked.

I looked at his tall, thin body and my own and decided we could both stand a few calories. "A banana split with everything, please."

Kimberly had picked up on Phil's remark. " 'Boss'? Is that a figure of speech, or have your parents decided to let you take over the business, Lisa?"

"Yes, they have. Randall's Bookstore is mine!" Phil and I began to talk at the same time, trying to tell them about our plans for the store. Steve looked a little blank, but Kimberly was almost as excited as we were.

"It should be simple for you to run it, Lisa," she cried.

"Well, I'm not expecting trouble, but making a profit is another thing."

Just then the atmosphere in Polly's changed, as if someone really special had just come in. Almost without looking, I sensed it was Meredith and Kevin. Then Meredith swept past us, her long, dark hair bouncing as she walked. Behind her, looking a little sullen, was Kevin. When he saw me, his face lit up and he stopped at our table.

"Hi, Lisa!" His gaze ran up and down my new outfit. "You look great." He nodded to Phil and Kimberly and Steve, but he kept on looking at me! "My mother loved the perfume bottle," he said. "Dad took her out to dinner, and she opened her gifts before they left."

Meredith's cool voice rang out loud and clear. "Here's a booth, Kevin. Are you coming?"

He scowled, and I decided things weren't going too well between those two that night. "Duty calls," he said. "See you guys." He flashed a beautiful smile at me. I willed myself not to blush, but inside I was so excited I could hardly contain myself. Kimberly noticed the exchange and raised an eyebrow at me.

The rest of the evening went by in a dream. I must have joined in the conversation and laughter because no one looked at me strangely. But all the time I felt like an actress. Every smile, every gesture was performed with Kevin in mind. I wanted him to think I was wonderfully interesting and that I was having the best time in the world. If I had to flirt with Phil in order to do that, so be it. Certainly Phil didn't seem to mind. He glowed in the attention I was giving him. Although my conscience was telling me how wrong I was to raise his hopes like that, I couldn't seem to stop myself.

Finally we got up to go, and I risked a glance at Kevin and Meredith. They were sitting there sulking. Meredith's eyes were fixed on the soda in her glass, and her pretty mouth was pouting. *She's probably drinking diet soda,* I thought, feeling a little guilty about the banana split. Trust Meredith not to put anything fattening into her gorgeous little body.

Kevin looked up, almost as though he felt me looking at him. He smiled at me again, that white-toothed, gorgeous smile, and I smiled back, a little tentatively. Meredith looked up, too, and flipped her hand at us. I'd seen her do that before. It was the way she waved to people who weren't important at all in her mind.

Outside, in the cool night, Phil and I said goodbye to Kimberly and Steve, who were going back to Kimberly's house to watch a new movie on cable TV. They invited us to go along, but I said I'd better get back home. After seeing Kevin I just didn't feel like being with my friends anymore. Funny, even though he was with Meredith, I didn't feel miserable as I had so many times before. There had been something different between us that day.

On the drive home, I didn't say much. Usually I enjoyed talking to Phil because he was so intelligent and often so funny. But that night his chatter didn't really register with me. I could think only of Kevin and the way he'd smiled at me.

"Hey," Phil said, glancing at me, "what world are you in, Lisa?"

I came to with a start. "I'm sorry, Phil. What did you say?"

"I said, when school's out in another couple of weeks, we can start in at the shop and really get ready for the summer trade. My mother said she'll ride to work with Dad, so I can use her car most days. That way, you and I can hit the sales and auctions to get new stock."

I laughed. "For a part-time employee, you're really planning a lot of work for yourself. I guess we'll have to go to the sales on days when my mother can stay in the store for a little while. That's the only problem with running a store—you have to be there for so many hours every day."

"That's OK. We'll manage. It'll be fun."

As we approached my house, I knew I should ask Phil in to watch the cable TV movie, but I really wanted to be alone with my thoughts of Kevin. Phil cut the engine, and we just sat there for a minute while I wrestled with my natural sense of hospitality. Finally, I decided to do the polite thing. "Want to come in and watch the movie?"

Phil smiled and said reluctantly, "I wish I could, but I promised Joey I'd come home and play a few video games with him. He's hooked on them these days."

"Well, thanks for the banana split and the ride. It was fun, Phil."

Before I realized what he was doing, he'd leaned over and kissed me, right on the mouth. I tried not to, but I couldn't help pulling away a little. I knew he felt it and was hurt, for he released me right away.

"Sorry, boss," he said quietly. "I forgot we're starting an employer-employee relationship."

I couldn't bear his unhappy frown, so I leaned over and kissed him lightly on the cheek. "That's to seal our new work agreement." And I was out the door before he could say a word.

Chapter Four

Sunday passed in a dream. I turned down Mom and Dad's invitation to go into Rochester for dinner and a movie. I wanted to be alone with my thoughts. Like a broken record, my mind kept repeating what Kevin had said to me. "You look great, you look great, you look great." His eyes had shown me he really thought it, too. Kimberly had said it was wishful thinking to imagine Meredith and Kevin breaking up, but even she had looked impressed when he'd singled me out at Polly's the previous evening.

"You're all ready for school?" my mother asked in disbelief when I entered the kitchen on Monday morning. "I can't believe it! You're always running to catch that bus."

I tried to look very serious. "I've turned over a new leaf, now that I'm the proprietor of a well-known bookshop and antique store." I wanted to make her laugh. I couldn't admit my real reason for being early. Mom was practical, like Kimberly.

It was the last week of classes before exam week, the last full week in which I'd have some chance of running into Kevin. I don't know what I was hoping for—just to see his face, I suppose, and to have him smile at me again. At the moment that seemed like enough. When you're as crazy about someone as I was about Kevin, you don't need much to keep the dreams stirring inside your head. I imagined us on the beach at Lake Ontario, turning golden tan in the summer sun; together at the prom the following year, dancing cheek to cheek; and passing a lonely, cast-off Meredith on the street, giving her pitying looks.

I knew all those scenes were totally unrealistic, but that didn't make them any less wonderful. Perhaps that was why I loved books and movies. It would take a dozen lifetimes to experience all the things that happen on the screen or in books.

"Hey," a laughing voice said in the hall before class. "Your mind may be on higher things, but you'd better watch where you're going. You almost walked right into me, do you know that?"

It was Kevin, looking like a movie star, his deep brown eyes sparkling. We were so close that I could smell his men's cologne. It wasn't overpowering like the kind some of the boys wore, the ones who wanted to make an impression on girls. It just smelled exotic and delicious.

From somewhere deep inside me, I dredged up a Meredith-type smile. I looked deep into Kevin's eyes with a flirty smile and said, "Thanks for watching out for me, Kevin."

His face got closer, and I could see specks of green in his eyes. I felt as though he were going to kiss me, right there in the hall at Central High, and my breathing became shallow. I could feel the blood mounting into my cheeks.

And then—nothing happened! Because a sharp, sarcastic voice said, "Lining them up, Kevin? I haven't left yet, you know." Meredith flung me a brief glance, and just by the way she looked at me, I knew she was dismissing me as any serious competition.

Hurriedly I clasped my books and notebook tighter, said, "See ya," in the direction of both of them, and went racing down the hall. All the way through Mr. Brentwood's English class, I went over and over that scene in my mind. Had Kevin been about to kiss me? And what had Meredith meant by saying she hadn't left yet?

All that last week of school, Kevin and I kept running into each other. Sometimes we'd smile at each other and say hi as we passed in the hallway. Occasionally he gave me a little nod and a wink. On Friday we stood in line together in the cafeteria, and as we talked, I could feel that there was something special between us.

Later, as I was finishing my tuna sandwich with Kimberly, I told her what I'd sensed. "Kimberly, I'm sure he likes me. He looks at me like I'm really special to him."

"You're crazy," Kimberly said, taking the last bite of her sandwich. "I run into him sometimes, too, but that doesn't mean he's madly in love with me."

"I know," I said, deflated. "But really, it's beginning to seem like fate."

She rolled up her eyes in despair. "Honestly, Lisa, when are you going to start separating the books you read from real life?"

"Never!" I said hotly. At that moment the bell rang, and I stormed out of the cafeteria without even saying goodbye.

That evening, as if to show me she was sorry for laughing at me, Kimberly came by my house with a batch of cookies she'd made. We sat on the back steps, drinking iced tea with mint and munching on the cookies.

"News for you," she said. "Through the grapevine, I hear that Meredith Hunt is going to Europe with her family this summer. Her brother Jerry is taking along his college room-mate, who is *really* handsome and very sophisticated. After all, he's a college sophomore."

"Who told you?" I was so excited, I spilled half my iced tea in the rhododendrons.

"I heard it from Mimi and Bonnie. I guess Meredith is bragging all over the place about Neil. That's her brother's roommate. And Kevin is pretty furious."

A little flame of hope shot up inside me again, but I didn't say anything, not after Kimberly's lecture in the cafeteria. We just went on discussing Meredith's summer vaca-tion, and we were both feeling a little envious. My summer in the bookshop seemed almost boring, now, beside this exciting trip, but then, I thought optimistically, Kevin would be in Kingsway.

The next week was exam week, and I didn't run into Kevin once. My tests never seemed to coincide with his. I did see quite a bit of Phil, though. He was itching for school to be over so we could get to work at the shop. One day when we both finished our English tests at the same time, he waited for me on the front steps of the school. "The buses won't be leaving for another forty-five minutes," he said. "Come over to Polly's for a Coke?"

"Sure," I said. "Thanks."

Polly's was only half full because most of the kids were still finishing exams. A quick glance around showed me Kevin wasn't there, so I relaxed and talked with Phil while we sipped our Cokes.

"I'm glad school's out," he said. "I like some of my classes, but everything gets to be a drag at this time of year."

"I know," I agreed, but I didn't really feel that way. Instead, I was kind of depressed knowing there wouldn't be much chance of running into Kevin during vacation. It's hard to keep a dream going for an entire summer without something to feed it.

"Lisa." Phil's voice sounded kind of funny, and when I looked up, I saw that his face was red.

"What's up, Phil?"

"Well, next Wednesday is the class picnic, and I just thought, if you don't already have a date, maybe you'd go with me."

A date? I didn't have one, and I did want to go to the picnic. There was no reason I shouldn't go with some of my girlfriends or with Kimberly and Steve. Lots of people would go in bunches. But it would be fun to go with a boy. Even if it was the wrong one.

I smiled at him and said, "I'd like that, Phil."

I was pretty sure Kevin and Meredith would be at the picnic together, but at least I'd have a chance to see him. Then I was ashamed of myself. Phil was so nice, and I knew he really liked me. How could I be so selfish? The fact was, I was leading him on. Well, I'd already accepted, and I wouldn't do something like that again. But I'd make sure we had fun at the picnic, and I gave him a really big smile. I'd go to the class picnic, and I'd give every ounce of my attention to the tall, lanky boy who was beaming at me so happily from across the table.

Chapter Five

The day of the class picnic turned out to be one of those beautiful June days that has inspired poets. In our climate a perfect June day is rare. Sometimes it's too hot, sometimes too cold, but this Wednesday was just right.

I wore a pair of white shorts, a sleeveless red blouse, and a couple of thin gold chains, which made my tiny bit of tan seem soft and rich. There's not much you can do with short, wavy, almost-blond hair, so I settled for a pair of gold earrings to match the highlights in my hair. I put on a bit of makeup and decided I looked my best. It was sure to be a wonderful day.

The picnic was held in a little grove of pine

trees on the top of a hill, and the view of the valley was breathtaking. There were two shelters, made of time-mellowed redwood, a few scattered picnic tables, four or five stone grills, and a drinking fountain. The picnic ground had been donated by a long-gone millionaire named Elias Fortescue, and the place was called, naturally enough, Fortescue Park. The teachers were in charge of cooking the hamburgers and hot dogs, and there were kegs of soda and big jars of relish, mustard, and ketchup. Almost everyone brought a contribution, a salad or cake or a bag of potato chips or pretzels.

I loved it. The whole place smelled of pine needles and wood smoke and broiling hamburgers. A tiny brook crept down the hillside, rippling over flat stones. We were early, and as we were waiting for everyone to arrive, Phil and I went over to the bank of the brook and watched the minnows darting through the water.

"This is really something!" Phil said enthusiastically. "Kingsway sure has Brooklyn Heights beat. I can't believe this beautiful spot is only five miles from home. Back in the city, we had to drive for at least an hour to find a little stream and a fantastic view like these."

"Phil, you really appreciate the simple things in life." It was true, too. He seemed to plunge wholeheartedly into every new experience.

"That's right. GIve me a sunny afternoon, a good friend, and a part-time job, and I'm completely happy. By the way, I heard about an auction in Greenville on Saturday. My mother said I could have her car, so I thought maybe we'd go hunt up some books and antiques. I mean, as long as you're not busy and your mother can stay at the store."

"Great, Phil," I said enthusiastically. "I've been thinking it's about time we got started with the store. And we could use some new stock. I'll ask Mom if she's free." Then I heard Steve yelling to us. "I suppose we'd better mingle. Almost everyone is here now, I think." But had the most important person come? I wondered.

We slipped down to the pine-needled path to the picnic tables and were greeted by our friends. Phil fit right in with them, even though he was a newcomer. He said it was easier being a new kid in a small-town high school than being a newcomer in a huge city school.

Finally the feast got started. We lined up to get hot dogs and hamburgers from the teachers. When I got to the front of the line, Mr. Brentwood, my English teacher, put a hamburger on my paper plate.

"White or red hot dog?" he asked me.

"White, please." I turned to Phil and said, "Try a white hot dog. We're famous for them in this part of the country."

Mr. Brentwood grinned and said, "She's right. Actually, I'm not sure they sell them in very many other areas of the United States."

Phil and I piled our plates with salad and chips and sat down on the wooden benches, which were fastened to the long picnic tables. Everything tasted wonderful. Somehow, hot dogs never taste as good when they're cooked in a pan on top of the stove.

After we'd eaten, some of the boys began to fool around, squirting soda at everyone, blowing straw wrappers around, and just generally acting silly.

Some of the girls were squealing and laughing and threatening the boys, but it was no big deal. That is, until I heard a loud, clear voice say, "Pete, you're a total idiot. Look what you've done to my blouse! I'll never get this stain out."

Meredith was down at the very end of our table, and she was standing with soda all over her pink blouse. Pete Humphrey, one of the class clowns, was standing opposite her, and his face was bright red. Even though I knew it must be maddening for Meredith to have a dark stain on a beautiful blouse, I felt sorry for Pete. Meredith just kept glaring at him.

Kevin was sitting at the table beside Meredith, looking both embarrassed and bored. She turned on him, then, and practically screamed, "Well, are you just going to sit there, Kevin?"

"What do you want me to do?" he asked, sighing.

"*Say* something to this jerk."

Kevin looked at Pete and drawled out, "You're a bad boy, Pete. Don't ever do that again!"

Everyone laughed, and Meredith stormed off to the rest room. A couple of her friends tagged along, to help rinse out the stain on her blouse, I assumed, and things got back to normal.

A gym teacher, Ms. Melton, jumped up on one of the benches and said, "After you dump everything in the trash cans, line up for the races."

"Races?" Phil asked.

Steve filled him in. "Potato sack races and relay races and Look-Ma-no-hands races, where you carry something in your teeth to the opposite side of the field. It's the crazy stuff we usually do at these picnics."

While we cleared the tables, I kept looking over in Kevin's direction, trying not to let him see me. I wondered whether he and Meredith were as annoyed with each other as they seemed to be. He certainly didn't look as though he was having a good time. And once again I thought, *Maybe they're breaking up. Maybe there really is a chance for me!*

Meredith didn't return for some time, and when she did, she was wearing a boy's light-weight jacket over her blouse. Personally I thought it might be better to let the hot sun dry up the damp spot on her blouse, but I guess she wanted everyone to realize just how awful the little accident had been.

"I don't usually go in for all these races," I said to Phil. "But go ahead if you want to. There'll be softball later, too."

"Oh, come on, Lisa," he said, his eyes sparkling. "How about trying just one race with me?"

I'm not the most coordinated person in the world. Maybe it's because I grew too fast, or maybe it's because I get nervous when I have to perform before people who are good athletes. But Phil looked so happy and excited about entering that I agreed. We decided to go for the three-legged race. Phil got a piece of rope from Ms. Melton, then bent down and tied his right leg to my left one. As we hobbled together toward the starting line, I glanced around for Kevin and Meredith. They were right behind us. I knew they'd do well in the race. Kevin is a star on the basketball team, and Meredith is a cheerleader.

When the starting gun went off, we all began hopping for the finish line on the other side of the open field. Since both Phil and I were tall, we did pretty well at first, loping along like a three-legged bunny. In fact, we outdistanced quite a few people, including Meredith and Kevin.

Then it happened. We weren't far from the end when my free foot sank into a hole. I turned my ankle, and both Phil and I went tumbling down. By that time several couples were at the finish line, and I knew we'd lost. At the moment, however, I didn't much care because my ankle was throbbing like crazy. I could feel tears welling up in my eyes.

Phil and I were both sitting on the ground, of course, and he immediately started untying our legs. "Are you OK, Lisa?" he kept asking. I think most boys would have been annoyed that a klutz had spoiled their chances of winning the race. But he seemed genuinely concerned about me, as if it didn't matter at all.

"I'm all right," I said, trying to smile. "But I don't think I can get up, Phil. I must have sprained my ankle."

A group of concerned teachers and

friends had gathered around us to see what had gone wrong, and Mrs. Sommers, the school nurse, came to look at my ankle. But I hardly noticed because all of a sudden Kevin was there. He crouched and put his arm around my shoulders. "Poor kid," he said. "Lean back against me."

Phil stood up quickly. Our legs were free by then, and his face paled under his early-summer tan. I knew he resented Kevin, but I didn't care. It was sheer heaven to lean back against that strong body, as I'd so often dreamed of doing. The pain ebbed, and I didn't care whether I seemed like a klutz or not. Mrs. Sommers finished checking my ankle and told me I'd either sprained it or pulled some tendons.

"We'll elevate your foot," she said. "And I'll wrap it in an Ace bandage. But you'd better see a doctor when you get home. I don't think you should stand on it, at least not for the time being. Would you two boys carry her back to the pavilion?" She smiled at Kevin and Phil.

I felt like a princess as they carried me back to the picnic area. They made a cradle for me with their hands, and I put one arm around each of their necks. As we passed her, I heard Meredith mutter, "Jerk!" I didn't know whether she meant Kevin or me, but it didn't really matter.

After the nurse had finished binding up my foot and ankle, I stretched out on one of the long benches. Kimberly brought me a glass of root beer, and she, Kevin, and Phil clustered around me.

"Do you want to go home?" Phil asked anxiously.

I shook my head. "No, thanks. I'm fine now. Go and play softball. The game's just about ready to start. I'll watch from here."

"Just call if you need anything," Kevin said. He and Phil went down the little knoll and out onto the field where the other kids were waiting to get the softball game started. I relaxed in the sun, trying not to smile at my wonderful secret thoughts.

"I'm beginning to think he does like you!" Kimberly said.

"Kimberly, do you think the saying is true—wishing makes it so? I've been wishing for months and months!"

"Well, if Meredith's going to Europe for the whole summer, maybe he thinks it's time to look around. Oh, here she comes."

"She," of course, was Meredith, who sat down at the table next to ours with some of her gang. She very pointedly did not ask me how my ankle was, so I fixed my attention on the softball game, which got to be pretty exciting. Meredith and her friends cheered for

Kevin's team, and Kimberly and I yelled for Phil's. I wouldn't have dared to do otherwise.

By the time Kevin's team won, it was just about time to go home. Already the sun, a great ball of fire, was starting to go down behind the hills, and everything was bathed in a brilliant orange light. Phil helped me hop out to the little creek for one last look at the darting minnows.

Phil drove home very carefully, avoiding all the worst bumps in the rutted country road that led from the picnic grounds. All in all, it had been a good day. I didn't even mind too much the fact that my ankle had swollen quite a bit and was hurting.

"Want me to take you to the doctor right away?" he asked.

"No, thanks. I'll wait till I get home. Mom will probably have some good old-fashioned remedy for a twisted ankle." As we pulled into our driveway, I suddenly had a terrible thought. "Phil, I planned to start full-time at the shop tomorrow. And there's the auction in Greenville on Saturday. What if I can't walk around by then?"

He smiled at me. "Not to worry. You have your able assistant, Phil Bradley. I'll do all the legwork." Then he leaned over and kissed me very gently. This time, I didn't make the mistake of pulling back. He was too nice and too thoughtful. I returned the kiss, but I couldn't help closing my eyes and pretending it was Kevin.

Chapter Six

The day after the picnic it rained. My ankle hurt, and I felt let down. Mom and Dad decided I'd better rest my foot for a few days, especially since Phil could take over the running of the bookstore.

"But, Dad," I protested, "I should be there. Phil doesn't know prices or where to look for things."

"Most of the prices are penciled in the books, and there are tags on the antiques," my father responded. "If he's not certain, he can call you. A few days' rest won't hurt that ankle."

So I sat around, bored and frustrated. Hanging around watching TV or reading with my leg propped up on a stool was not my idea of the perfect way to start my summer vacation. And, of course, I kept hoping against hope that Kevin would call, just to see how my ankle was. But he didn't.

Kimberly visited me every day, bringing magazines and date nut squares from a nearby bakery. She kept me posted on everything that was going on, too, which was great because I felt cut off from the outside world. On Friday she came in, dropped onto the couch beside me, and announced, "She's gone. Meredith has left for New York City and then for Europe."

I sat up straight. "I can't believe it! I thought something would happen to keep her in Kingsway. How did you find out?"

"My mother was in the post office in Bragdon, and Mrs. Holden told her." Mrs. Holden lived next door to the Hunts, so she was in a position to know. "Honestly, Lisa, I'm beginning to think something really could happen between you and Kevin."

Kimberly's words sent a flood of warmth right through me. "That must be why Meredith and Kevin were quarreling so much the last couple of weeks. I suppose he resents her going off to Europe with her brother's handsome friend along." I sighed and shifted my foot a little. "But he hasn't called me,

Kimberly. Maybe I'm just imagining things, as usual."

She laughed. "Do not despair, my wounded friend. After he thinks things over, Kevin may decide you're the one for him."

"Don't I wish."

"Absence doesn't necessarily make the heart grow fonder, you know."

Right then I began to make my plans. My ankle was getting better. I could bear most of my weight on it by now, and I maneuvered my way around with the help of an old wooden cane Dad used years before when he had broken his toe. Saturday I'd go into the shop and mind the store. Phil would have to go to the Greenville auction on his own. Maybe Kevin had been stopping at the store to see me instead of calling me at home. The next day, I wouldn't miss his visit.

After Kimberly left, I talked to my mother about going back to work. "I think you should stay off it for a few more days," she said.

"Mom, I'm going stir crazy. I won't have to walk around much tomorrow. If we have a hundred customers, I'll send up flares. You and Dad just go on into the city and see the dentist and do all the things you have to do."

So the next day Dad gave Phil a list of instructions a mile long of what to look for at the auction. Mom fixed a table for me on the store's porch with a big pitcher of ice water, aspirin in case my ankle hurt, and a few little snacks. They went off to Rochester, and I waved to Phil as he drove away for the auction in his mother's car. I sat back to wait for customers.

I was working on a card file listing all the authors we had in stock, and that kept me occupied. The traffic wasn't very heavy, but I had a few browsers and buyers. The store even got quite busy at one point. Obviously I hadn't done all that much damage to my foot because I was able to hobble around quite easily now. My customers were very understanding.

When things slowed down a little, I went back to my seat on the porch and propped up my foot. The ice water tasted wonderful. I nibbled at the cheese and peanut-butter crackers and soaked up the warm, beautiful sunshine while I transcribed my handwritten list onto file cards. I printed these carefully, one author to a card, while I thought wistfully of how fast a computer would have entered all this information.

I was really engrossed in my job when a car pulled up in front of the store. I looked up casually. Then my heart leaped like a bird, and my breath caught somewhere in my throat. It was Kevin!

"Hi, Lisa. I thought I'd drop in and see

how that ankle's coming along," he said as he got out of the car. "I meant to call and check on you, but things have been hectic the last few days."

I knew what that meant. He had been seeing Meredith off to New York or partying with her before she left or just plain fighting with her because she was going. But I didn't care. He was here now, and that's all that mattered to me. I could feel the corners of my mouth turning up uncontrollably.

I invited him to sit on the porch, and he sat down on an antique wooden rocker that was for sale. "How did you know I was here?" I asked.

"I stopped at your house, and no one was there, so I figured you were probably here."

He had stopped at my house! I couldn't believe it. Yet it had happened, and the living proof was sitting right there on the porch of my bookshop.

We chatted for a while, which was surprisingly easy because Kevin was so casual and sure of himself. He was never at a loss for words. I envied him that quality. Of course when I'm talking to Kimberly or Phil and I'm relaxed, I can talk a mile a minute. But at a large party, or with people like Meredith's crowd, people who have been around so much more than I have, I become tongue-tied and very, very shy.

"This is just ice water," I said, "but there's soda in the fridge, if you'd like some."

"Great," he said. When I started to struggle to my feet, he put a hand on my shoulder. My skin tingled beneath the silky cotton blouse I was wearing. "Stay where you are," he ordered. "You shouldn't be walking around on that ankle. I can find the kitchen without a compass, you know."

He brought back Cokes for both of us, and I just sat there basking in the warmth of his company. I felt as if I were living in a book, one in which love and romance are the most important things in life and everything comes out right in the end.

Finally he said casually, "I guess you know that Meredith has been my girlfriend. But we've been arguing a lot lately." He smiled and I thought he didn't seem the least bit upset. "We broke up right before she left, and I wondered if you'd consider going out to dinner with me next Saturday. Your ankle will be OK by then, won't it?"

I blinked hard. Was this dream of mine really coming true? I looked into Kevin's deep brown eyes and smiled. "Sure, to both questions."

"That's great, Lisa. Ever since that day I

58

stopped to buy my mother's birthday gift, I've been thinking about you. You get excited about things, not the way some girls act so bored. I like that."

I couldn't find the words, so I just smiled at him. I couldn't tell him that I'd been thinking of him a lot longer than that.

He leaned over and touched my wavy, dark-blond hair. "Your hair is so soft and old-fashioned, like you are."

I laughed. "I'm not sure whether that's a compliment or not."

His eyes, so close to mine, were like brown velvet. "Believe me, it's a compliment." Then he kissed me lightly, as though he didn't want to frighten me. It was a delicious kiss, more wonderful than any I'd ever had before. His lips were warm and gentle, and there was no hint of the sophisticated, experienced boy I had imagined him to be. "You're so sweet, Lisa," he murmured. "It's nice to be with a girl who's completely herself. I don't think there's a phony bone in your body."

He was about to kiss me again when a car pulled up. "Oops, that must be a customer," I said, pulling away reluctantly.

Phil came bouncing up the steps, his face beaming. He didn't even notice Kevin and began talking to me, his voice brimming with enthusiasm. "Wait till you see the good buys I got at that auction! There were a few antiques and a bunch of great children's books. I know you said one of your regular customers is always looking for good children's books for her collection."

"That's marvelous, Phil! I knew you were going to be an asset to this corporation!"

"Phil's working with you, Lisa?" Kevin didn't sound too pleased.

Phil glanced at him, seeing him for the first time. He replied, his voice light, "I'm her new assistant." He looked at my propped-up foot. "And a good thing she has me right now. I'm the feet of the company, I think you could say."

Kevin smiled uncomfortably. "I guess she has the right assistant. You sound like you know what you're doing. I sure wouldn't be much help. About all I can do for Lisa is bring her a can of Coke."

Wow! Was that me these two attractive boys were talking about? With two handsome men paying attention to me, I felt like the heroine in a movie. It was the first time in my whole life that such a thing had happened. I knew that these two boys even resented each other somewhat, and all because of me. It gave me a sensation of power I'd never felt before. This was probably the way Meredith felt all the time.

Kevin looked at his watch. "Guess I'd better go. My mother's having guests for dinner, so I have to be on time." He started down the steps, then turned to give me his charming smile again. "Get well, Lisa. I'll see you next Saturday, if not before. Eight o'clock?"

"Eight o'clock," I said, my voice coming out in a whisper.

He left then, and I turned to Phil, who was unloading his car. He'd piled a few books, a Victorian table croquet set, and two china dolls on the porch so I could look them over. But all the excitement had left him, and it didn't take much imagination to see that Kevin had spoiled his happy mood. I felt really guilty, although I'd certainly never pretended to be romantically interested in Phil Bradley. Still, I knew how it felt to want someone who doesn't want you.

But now he does, I thought excitedly. *Wishing really does make it so.* I looked over at Phil, his head bent over an old copy of *Winnie the Pooh. Don't wish for me, Phil,* I thought. *Wish for someone wonderful, someone who really deserves you.*

He looked up at me, saw me watching him, and his face became concerned. "What's the matter, Lisa? You're crying."

I realized then that my eyes were full of tears, tears for Phil, my friend. I said hastily, "My ankle started hurting again, that's all."

Chapter Seven

The next week crawled by, even though my ankle began to feel better. On Tuesday Phil and I started making plans for the bookshop, trying to draw in more customers. But the only thing that mattered, of course, was my Saturday night date with Kevin. *Why me?* I kept asking myself. *What have I done to deserve this?*

"So do you have any advertising ideas, Lisa?" Phil asked in his practical voice.

I'd been imagining what it would feel like to be wrapped up in Kevin's strong arms. "Uh, what did you say, Phil?"

"Hey, wake up, dreamer," he said, grinning. "Your business is going to go bust if you insist on keeping your head in the clouds."

Phil would have been livid if he had known what I'd really been thinking about. "Actually, I've been giving it a lot of thought," I said in my businesslike voice. "We could put up a nice wooden sign just before the turnoff onto the expressway. Lots of tourists would make the detour to Kingsway to get a look at an old bookshop if they only knew about it."

"Great, but we'll have to get permission from whoever owns the land."

"That's Mr. Simpkins," I said. "I know he'll let us do it. He's an old friend of my father's."

That evening Dad called Mr. Simpkins and got permission to put up a sign, and the next day Phil got out wood, a hammer, and nails. In no time he had hand lettered a beautiful sign with the name of the store on it and directions where to turn. Then he varnished the sign, and it looked very attractive.

"*I'd* turn off here, if I saw that sign," I told him.

"I think there's something about a sign advertising a bookstore out in the country that will attract collectors," he said.

And he was right. Business began to pick up a little on Thursday after he put the sign up. He'd done a beautiful job, and I really appreciated his help. That wasn't all he did, either. Since I was still hopping around like a stork, he dusted the books and rearranged the cases of antiques for me.

Mom and Dad were really pleased with him, too. Thursday night as we were eating dinner out on the back porch, Dad said approvingly, "I think you and Phil are doing a great job, Lisa. That young man has a feel for books and antiques."

"He loves them, that's why," I told him. "I think he cares about the store almost as much as I do."

My mother threw me a little sidelong glance. "You and Phil have a lot in common. Why don't you invite him to dinner some night after you close up shop? You can ask Kimberly and Steve, too."

At first I was going to answer indignantly because I knew she was matchmaking and I didn't want to be matched up with Phil. But then, too, I didn't want to say anything about Kevin, so I merely said, "I might do that."

My parents knew I was going out with Kevin on Saturday night, and they hadn't said anything against it, but I had the distinct feeling that they didn't really approve. When I thought about it, I got a little angry. The reason for their resentment was that Kevin ran with a more sophisticated, wealthier crowd. Anyway, it was only Kevin himself I had to worry about, not his crowd, and he was nice and friendly and not a show-off.

Saturday finally came, and I closed the store at six sharp, waiting impatiently for Phil to get his stuff together. Although my ankle was in good shape by then, he insisted on driving me home. I couldn't help noticing he was kind of quiet, but I pretended things were perfectly normal. I talked to him about our work at the store. Inside, of course, I was thinking about anything but. I just wanted to get home, have a shower, and get ready for my date with Kevin.

As we reached my house, I said hastily, "Thanks so much for bringing me home, Phil. See you on Monday, OK? Dad's going to take over tomorrow."

"Sure. Have a good weekend." He looked really unhappy, but I just couldn't think about that.

I hopped out of the car and almost skipped into the house. I shouted hello to my parents, then went upstairs to get ready. Dinner at eight! That sounded so elegant and grown-up to me. Dinner at our house was at six, with an occasional one at seven if we had guests or were busy. I wondered where we would go, but decided I could safely leave that to Kevin, who apparently spent more time in

Rochester than he did in Bragdon or Kingsway.

I took a shower and washed my hair. The nice thing about having shoulder-length hair was that it was quick to dry. It was too short just now to set in any glamorous way, but that couldn't be helped. I decided I'd let it grow out.

I put on a beautiful, silky, pink dress with a fitted waist and a full, flowing skirt. I'd saved the money Grandma Randall had sent me for my birthday, and I'd bought the dress the last time I'd gone into Rochester. I just loved it, and I think it loved me because it fit in all the right places, and the color made me seem to glow. Or perhaps that was because I was so happy and excited.

By now I had a little tan, so I smoothed on some darker blusher, did my eyes very carefully, and added lip gloss. While my hair was still damp, I brushed it so that it fell in soft waves around my face. Dangly gold earrings, a gift from my mother, added a touch of glamour. I was ready, and it was only a little after seven o'clock, so I decided to call Kimberly.

"All set for your dinner date?" she asked.

"As set as I'll ever be. I wish I had long, black hair and didn't look so darned wholesome!"

She laughed. "I guess you and I aren't

sophisticated types. Maybe we'll outgrow it some day."

"Yeah, but my date with Kevin is tonight!" I said, laughing.

We talked for a while. Kimberly told me she'd seen Phil at the drugstore and that he'd looked a little sad, she thought. I felt a twinge of conscience. "He's fun to work with," I said. "He loves books just as much as I do."

But I really couldn't think of Phil at that exciting moment. I said goodbye to Kimberly, then checked out my clothes, hair, and makeup one more time. When I heard the doorbell ring, I thought my heart would burst. I could hear my breath, shallow, quick, and uneven, so I tried to take deep breaths to calm down. I wanted to seem normal when I went downstairs. *It's only a date, Lisa Randall*, I told myself. But I knew that wasn't true. I hadn't felt like this the night Phil took me to Polly's for ice cream. I'd been calm and light-hearted. But I couldn't make myself be that way when Kevin was my date.

Mom called up to me, and I walked downstairs as casually as possible. Kevin was waiting in the entryway. He looked up at me and smiled. "You're beautiful, Lisa!"

He was absolutely gorgeous himself. His dark, wavy hair and brown eyes were set off by a creamy white suit. His shirt was pale blue with tiny pinstripes, and he wore a tie. *He's like a young Tom Selleck*, I thought as I smiled at him. He wasn't your average boy from Central High, that was for sure. Most of them wouldn't be caught dead in a suit, except at a wedding, much less wear one on a date.

My parents seemed favorably impressed, too, and I gave my mother a triumphant look. She had misjudged him, just because of gossip. After all, she'd always taught me not to judge people by hearsay.

"Drive carefully," Mom said as she waved us away.

"Have a good time," Dad called.

Kevin helped me into his father's car, a beautiful new Lincoln. Riding in that car beside Kevin, I felt so special. My dress, my white sandals, my careful makeup made me feel glamorous and grown-up, part of Kevin's wealthy, chic world.

The sun was just beginning to set in the west as we drove toward the city. The sun itself was pinky orange, like the material of my dress, and the sky was streaked with purple and red. It was as if we were riding in a chariot, straight into some brilliant and strange kingdom. Kevin was the prince, and I was the princess in a wonderful fairy tale. I held my breath, not wanting to disturb this rare vision.

"Lisa?" I smiled at him dreamily, and Kevin continued, "You look hypnotized by the sunset."

"I am."

"I thought we'd have dinner at the Changing Scene, if that's all right with you."

"That sounds just right," I said. Of course I didn't tell him I'd never been there before, and that I'd always longed to go.

By the time we arrived at the restaurant and were seated, the dusk had turned velvety dark, and the golden lights pierced that darkness like so many shiny stickpins. We had a view of the lights on the river, and the sight was breathtaking. Colored lights were reflected on the shiny, dark surface of the water. "It's so beautiful," I said to Kevin. "Thank you for bringing me here."

He reached over and took one of my hands in his. "I wanted to take you somewhere special on our first date," he said.

"This is perfect." Our first date! That meant he planned on there being a second one. I couldn't have moved my hand from his if my life had depended on it.

We had shrimp cocktail and after that steak and baked potatoes with sour cream and chives, plus a marvelous salad, and delectable pastries for dessert. I was horrified at what it must have cost, but Kevin didn't seem to care. When the bill came, he just paid it, left a big tip, and asked me if I'd like more coffee. I shook my head. I'm not that keen on coffee.

We went to see a really hilarious Woody Allen movie after that. Because I was so full of delicious dinner, I was afraid I might fall asleep—but I didn't, of course. I had never been so vibrantly awake in my whole life. Kevin held my hand all during the film.

I hated having the movie end. But when it eventually did and we emerged from the dark theater into the lobby, we were both a little blinded by the brilliant light.

"Ooh, I always hate the way my eyes feel when I walk out of a dark theater," I told him as I rubbed my eyes. "But the movie was excellent."

"Yeah, Woody Allen's really funny. I love going to movies. I could see one every night."

"Movies are all right, but sometimes I love to spend an evening curled up with a good book."

"There's more to life than books, Lisa."

Normally Kevin would have gotten an argument from me, but I didn't want to spoil the mood. It's a good thing I didn't say anything because he added quickly, "Do you think you could tear yourself away from your

71

books and your shop to go out with me next Saturday night?"

I almost blurted out, "Do you really mean it?" but I forced myself to remain composed. Thinking of how Meredith would handle herself, I turned to him and said, "I'd love to, Kevin."

The Colonial Theatre had lots of paintings and sketches on the walls of the lobby, pictures done by local artists. Kevin and I looked at all of them, praising some, turning up our noses at others. I was so happy we had the same tastes in artists. We were laughing a lot at one particularly terrible painting of a man and a woman kissing when I backed into someone.

"Phil!"

"Oh, hi, Lisa. Small world." He smiled tightly at Kevin, then introduced his date, Betsy Farrell. She was a small girl with wheat-colored hair, kind of shy and sweet and very nice. I was surprised to find myself resenting her. Somehow I had thought that Phil was at home in Kingsway, watching TV or playing computer games with his little brother Joey. I certainly hadn't expected him to be out enjoying himself with a girl who wasn't me!

He looked really handsome, in nice blue jeans and a blue knit shirt that made his eyes even bluer.

"What did you think of the movie?" he asked me as Kevin and Betsy inspected a sketch of some wild horses.

"Loved it. I adore Woody Allen."

We went on talking for a few minutes, but the conversation seemed stiff, as though we were mere acquaintances, rather than friends and coworkers. The whole thing made me feel so bad that I just wanted to get away, so I excused myself to go to the rest room.

Combing my hair in front of the huge mirror, I looked at myself as if I were a stranger. I renewed my makeup, which now seemed too smooth and sophisticated. I began to wish I were at home, safe in my room, instead of in this brightly lit theater.

What was the matter with me? I'd been having such a wonderful time until Phil and Betsy had turned up. Why should I feel bad about Phil having a good time? But that's how I felt, and I was ashamed to face the fact. Maybe the evening had been a strain on me because I was trying so hard to live up to Kevin's kind of date. After all, he was used to girls like Meredith Hunt.

When I went back to the lobby, Kevin was still inspecting the pictures, and Phil and Betsy had gone. We went out into the June night, which had turned chilly and a little misty. When we got to the car in the parking lot, Kevin stopped me and pulled me to him. His lips were warm and firm against mine, and I knew that he was far more used to kissing than I was—but it didn't matter. I loved his kisses. They made me forget all my troubled thoughts of Phil.

I'd dreamed of this, but even in my dreams, I hadn't really been able to imagine what Kevin's kisses would be like. The few kisses I'd experienced had been very dull compared to these.

Kevin drove fast once we'd left the city. The road to Kingsway was narrow and dark, and trees and bushes leaned into the road, making the ride seem mysterious and dangerous. I really wished he'd slow down, but I didn't say anything. I was sure he knew how to drive, anyway, so I relaxed. With one arm around my shoulders, he drove casually, and I leaned back against his chest. I loved feeling his heart, regular and strong, beating against my ear. We were enclosed in a little world all our own, and I was deliriously happy. *I'm flying*, I thought, *just flying*. I didn't want to trade places with anyone in the whole world.

Kingsway was quiet, not a soul outside, and the dim lights barely lit up the sidewalks of the main street. There were lights on upstairs in my house, and the porch light was on, too. That was my parents' way of welcoming me home without saying, "See, we stayed up to wait for you." I knew they were reading or watching TV in their bedroom and that my mother's anxious ear would be tuned toward the street, waiting for Kevin's car to pull up.

In the darkness of the car, Kevin wrapped his arms around me, and his lips found mine. I tried my best not to tremble with happiness. "Thank you for a wonderful evening," I whispered.

"Thank *you*, Lisa. I enjoyed every minute of it, especially this." And he kissed me again. He kept on kissing me, more and more urgently.

Finally I pushed him away gently. "It's one o'clock. I—I suppose I'd better go in."

His hand caressed my jawline in a way that melted my bones. "I wish you didn't have to leave," he murmured. "I like you so much, Lisa."

"I like you, too." It came out in a whisper. I wanted to say, "I love you," but I knew that would be silly on a first date. "I really have to go now," I said. "Thanks again, Kevin. I had a really great time."

"I'll walk you to the door." He hopped out of the car and came around to my side. As we went up to the porch, he said, "I'll probably drop in at your bookshop sometime during the week, if that's OK. And, of course, there's

75

next Saturday. I'll think of someplace fun to go."

"I'm sure you will," I answered.

He kissed me again, then went down the steps while I let myself into the house. I felt like I was in one of those old movies you see on television where the heroine dances around in a filmy white gown because she's deliriously, happily in love.

I floated up the stairs and into my bedroom, and I didn't even put on the light. I just wanted to get into bed and think about the evening and about Kevin's kisses.

Chapter Eight

Monday, when Phil and I met at the shop, we didn't say much about Saturday night. It was as though we'd made some kind of agreement not to talk about each other's dates. It felt strange. Ever since I'd known Phil, we'd been comfortable with each other. And now we were acting jealous. But then I told myself that was silly. I'd wanted to go out with Kevin, wanted him interested in me for so long, and it was all finally happening.

"There's a big estate sale in Newfield tomorrow," Phil said to me during the afternoon. "Want to go?"

"If my mother can stay here, sure," I said. I did want to go, but in the back of my mind I was worried that I might miss Kevin if he stopped by to see me. I knew there was no way to tell Phil that I wanted to hang around the bookstore in case Kevin dropped by, so I made the arrangements with my mother. It wasn't one of her working days.

When Phil and I set off in his mother's ancient car Tuesday, I was definitely excited. It was the first time I'd gone on a buying expedition without my father. Up until then, he'd made the final decisions on what to buy—although he often asked my opinion on books and antiques.

Phil was a slower, more careful driver than Kevin, and I couldn't help feeling safer with him as we drove down the twisty, hilly dirt roads. We hadn't had much rain during that month, and that day was no exception. It was hot and dry. I smiled happily at Phil, and he smiled back. "Great day, huh?" he said.

"Definitely."

When we got to the Swann home in Newfield, there were dozens of people wandering around, examining the furniture and antiques. We were too late for the preview of antique furniture, but it didn't matter much. We couldn't afford to buy the expensive stuff. It was wonderful outdoors. The place smelled of new-mown grass, and everyone had a charmed, easygoing look. A little old gramophone was grinding out tinny, sweet music, and I heard a few people humming along. It seemed as if everyone had decided to push aside all worries and problems and just enjoy the day.

Phil and I looked at each other and grinned. We didn't have to say it—we somehow *knew* this was a magic day and we weren't to think of anything except the present. We walked around and looked at old postcards, buttons, and other trinkets. We bought some old buttonhooks and bottles, also some costume jewelry and baskets. These were things we were pretty sure would sell at the store.

"Let's go inside and look around," Phil said finally. "That's where the books probably are. There certainly aren't many out here."

The house was a stuffy old Victorian mansion with fireplaces in every room, marble-tiled bathrooms, and beautiful old wood paneling. There was a library, but all the books had been taken off the dark oak shelves and packed into big cardboard cartons. Phil went off to look for the woman who was conducting the book sale, while I looked at the books on the top layers of the boxes.

When Phil came back and quoted the price for each carton of books, I gasped with delight. "At that price, we can afford a lot of them! And there are a few pretty good ones in a couple of these boxes."

So, beaming like a pair of real money grubbers, we paid for the books and lifted them into Phil's car. Then we went back and bought glasses of tart lemonade from a refreshment stand someone had set up on the grounds.

"I think I'm going to like being the proprietor of a bookshop!" I told Phil.

"I already like being the assistant to the proprietor of a bookshop." The sun had burned Phil's straight nose and his cheeks, and he looked, I thought, like an all-American boy. I wondered if Betsy Farrell liked him a lot. It wouldn't be difficult for any girl to fall in love with him, I decided. I wanted to ask him if he liked Betsy, or if she'd been just a date to him, but I didn't dare. He hadn't mentioned Kevin's name to me, so I couldn't very well intrude upon his private life.

On the way home we talked excitedly about our finds of the day. We could hardly wait to get back to the store to unpack the books. "Every day is like Christmas when you're in this business, Phil. I just love it. I'm probably doomed to be a penniless bookseller all my life, instead of going into computer science or something practical."

"Nothing wrong with that." He paused to reflect, then said, "Someday I'd like to be a writer." He'd never said that before, and I felt as though he were sharing a deep secret with me.

I looked at him with real interest. "That would be wonderful, Phil. I'll sell your books in my shop!"

The ride home was beautiful, but as we got closer to Kingsway, I began to get more and more anxious. Up until then I'd been enjoying the afternoon with Phil, but now I was impatient to get back to Randall's Bookstore and Antique Shop to find out whether my mother had had a visit from Kevin. The trip began to seem like a slow-motion journey, and I began to blank Phil right out of my mind. I could hear his voice going on, and I suppose I must have answered fairly sensibly because he didn't give me any bewildered looks, but I wasn't really there. All I could think of was the past Saturday night, Kevin's wonderful kisses, and our next date.

I didn't think Phil noticed, but I was wrong. As we got closer to Kingsway, he said, sounding almost irritable, "Sometimes I get the feeling you're really out of it, Lisa. You've been gone for the last half hour."

I suppose I cover up guilt with anger because I snapped, "Stop analyzing me, Phil.

I'm entitled to my own thoughts once in a while."

His face flushed a dull red, and he clamped his lips together. I knew he was mad at me.

"Sorry," he said stiffly and kept his eyes on the road all the rest of the way.

When we pulled up in front of the store, I saw my mother talking to Kevin! Somehow I'd known he'd be there. Phil saw him, too, of course, and glanced at me as if to say, "So that's why you were so absentminded." But he greeted my mother and Kevin pleasantly. The two boys unloaded the boxes of books while I took in the small bags of antiques. Mom took a quick look at what we'd bought, said she liked it all, and then went home.

Once inside the store, I ran into the bathroom and washed my grimy face. I pulled a brush through my wavy hair and put on fresh makeup. Then I went out into the main room of the store and asked the boys if they'd like something to drink.

"Coke, please," Kevin said.

"Nothing for me, thanks. I've got to get on home if you don't need me any longer, Lisa." Phil's words were courteous, but I'd gotten to know him well these past months. He was hurt or angry or both. Unexpectedly, I felt a lump rising in my throat. I hadn't meant to snap at him like that. After all, he was one of my closest friends. But I let him leave without saying anything more than goodbye to him.

Chapter Nine

After that first Saturday night, my romance with Kevin blossomed. We began seeing each other two or three times a week. I felt like the heroine in a romantic English novel, the kind in which the poor governess meets the handsome rich man who falls in love with her by the end of the book. Mom said I had a *Jane Eyre* complex, but I didn't care. I thought it was absolutely thrilling to have the hero turn down the snobbish, rich beauty and find true love in the arms of the simple heroine. She always seemed plain at first, but once she fell in love, she was really beautiful.

Naturally, in my mind, Meredith was the snobbish, rich beauty, and I was the soon-to-be-gorgeous heroine.

Well, the first half of that plot was certainly true, and I planned to work on the second half, me. With Kevin around, I began to feel like a completely different person. For one thing, since he dropped in at the shop quite often, I started to wear makeup during the day and to dress in nice shorts and tops instead of the cutoff jeans and old blouses I'd worn before. The expensive new outfits weren't really as suitable as the old ones because my job was a dusty one, but I couldn't let him see me looking less than terrific.

Sometimes Kimberly stopped by for a few hours, and her joking comments about my new style made me feel a little self-conscious. "Well, I told you I was tired of looking like a grubby kid!" I said defensively. "And Kevin isn't used to slobs, you know." The unspoken thought was there. He was used to Meredith, who always looked as though she had stepped straight out of a TV commercial.

But in all fairness to Kevin, he never made me feel like I was a poor substitute for Meredith. He made wonderful arrangements for all our dates, and everything he planned was fun. Kevin's idea of a good time, I found out, was to go to dinner at an expensive restaurant and then sometimes to a movie. Whatever we did, each date always ended with long, long kisses in the front seat of his car. Obviously my relative inexperience hadn't bothered him in the least.

Sometimes we went places in the daytime, too. Brimming with charm, Kevin would stop at the store and say, "Do you think your assistant could stay in the shop while we take a drive?" There was no way I could say no to that, especially since I knew I was leaving the store in Phil's able hands.

I liked those excursions. As we drove along winding side roads, I could smell the ripening fruit. Everything looked bright and beautiful. It was then that I wished the summer would go on on forever, that Kevin and I could always be together just like this, and that I didn't have to worry about Meredith's coming back home.

There was one thing I didn't have to worry about, however—the shop. Phil was an even better assistant than I was when I was helping my parents. He used his mother's car to go to sales and auctions. Sometimes he went alone while I was watching the store. But most of the time we went together, spending hour upon hour grubbing through cardboard cartons of books, smiling with delight when we unearthed little treasures.

I liked the way Phil handled books, as though they were alive, almost. And when I said to him one day, "I like TV and movies, but with books you can imagine the characters just the way you want them to be," he nodded seriously.

"Right. And if you want to go back and read a couple of pages over again, you can do it. With TV it's gone—unless you have a video recorder, of course!" We'd smiled at each other with understanding.

Phil and I did a lot of work together. I was determined to make the shop profitable, and so was he. I just couldn't bear the idea of having Randall's sold to a stranger, someone who would come in and make drastic changes. I wanted it to be successful without changing any of its charm. I knew Phil felt the way I did about the store, and that made me feel very tender toward him.

The summer slipped by magically, each week consisting of dates with Kevin, visits with Kevin, work in the shop, and estate and garage sales. One summer afternoon followed another, and everything seemed almost other worldly. Before I knew it, it was the middle of August.

On the third Saturday in August, Kevin and I had made a date to go to the Rock Inn, a large, barnlike disco halfway between Bragdon and Rochester. When I got ready to go, I looked in the mirror and decided this wasn't the same Lisa Randall I'd known at the beginning of the summer. For one thing, I was thinner—and I'd never been exactly round. My cheeks had hollows in them because I wasn't getting enough rest; between days at the shop and evenings rushing around with Kevin, I'd nearly forgotten what my bed looked like. My mother constantly nagged me about that. My face also looked more grown-up and sophisticated. I was using makeup more subtly than I had before. I'd let my hair grow longer so that I was able to sweep it away from my tanned face, and that made me look older, too.

For the date at the Rock Inn, I'd bought a black silk dress that left one shoulder bare. My mother hadn't approved of it. "It's too old and too—sexy for you!" she said. Then she'd added reluctantly, "But it is very flattering! I can't blame you for buying it, Lisa. Every girl wants a sleek black dress. I did, too, when I was your age." She'd sighed. "It's just that I hate to have you grow up so soon!"

The dress was perfect for dancing, and that's why I'd bought it. The black high-heeled sandals made my feet ache a bit, but the total effect was worth it. Kevin whistled when he saw me. "Wow! You're too much for these parts. I wish we were going to New York to a really fancy club."

"Fat chance," I said. "I'm lucky my parents are letting me go to the Rock Inn."

Kevin laughed and stuck his head in the living room to say cheerfully, "Good night, Mrs. Randall, Mr. Randall. We'll try not to be too late." He seemed to know exactly what to say to them; he was polite but self-confident.

As usual on a Saturday night, Kevin had his parents' Lincoln. His own car was a secondhand blue Nissan Sentra, which he was nursing along until graduation, when his dad had promised him a new car. But his parents had two other cars, so Kevin usually took the Lincoln when we went out.

I had come to realize that Kevin liked to live life in the fast lane. Just the way he drove showed me that. Sometimes it took my breath away, and I wanted to beg him to slow down, but I didn't dare. I didn't want him to think I was just a timid, small-town girl—which I was! On that Saturday night we went barreling along the narrow secondary road toward the Rock Inn. It was a beautiful summer's night, but I was glad when we arrived safely.

The Rock Inn was very popular with people from the city and the surrounding towns. It was always crowded and noisy. And that night a blast of sound greeted us as we entered. It was exciting, there was no denying that. Even though I don't like loud noise much, I was soon caught up in the excitement. The colored lights, which swept over the dancers, made everyone seem larger than life, almost unreal.

"I'm not very good at this, you know," I told Kevin as we danced.

"You're fine," Kevin said, and in a way I was, because he was so good that I picked up on his energy.

When one of the really fast numbers ended, we sat down to have soft drinks. Our wooden table up on the balcony seated four, and since it was terribly crowded, another couple quickly joined us.

"Oh, hi, Kevin!" a voice drawled. It was Sharon James, one of Meredith's best friends, and her date. She gave me a look she might have given to a bug she'd discovered on a restroom wall. "Hi—" She hesitated, even though she had to know my name. We were in the same French class.

I could feel my face flaming, but I said sweetly in French, "*Je m'appelle Lisa*," which means, "My name is Lisa."

Kevin seemed just a little bit flustered, which was unusual for him. "Hello, Sharon. Hello, Tony."

They were old friends, of course, and they had lots to talk about. I couldn't think of much to say to Sharon, and obviously she didn't want to talk to me, so we both sat there, drinking our Cokes and listening to the boys.

Finally there was a pause in the conversation, and I thought we were about to go back to the dance floor, when Sharon's face brightened and she said, "You know Meredith is coming back from Europe next week, don't you, Kevin? She wrote me that she's going to throw a big party before her brother goes back to college." I could feel the unspoken words, "and his handsome roommate."

"That's nice," Kevin said. "I hope she'll invite Lisa and me."

There was suppressed fury on Sharon's face. That wasn't what she had expected to hear. "I imagine she's inviting all her old friends," she said. "Let's go back and dance, Tony."

After they'd gone, we went back to the dance floor, too, and were soon caught up in the music and the action. Perhaps it was because I was so unsure of myself with Kevin, but it seemed to me that he was quieter after that. My heart felt like a lump of putty somewhere in my chest. Had that whole summer been just an interlude for Kevin? Had seeing Meredith's friend and hearing her name brought him back to reality?

We danced for another half hour, then he

said abruptly, "Do you want to go? This is getting boring."

"If you want to." I was afraid I was going to cry, but Kevin didn't seem to notice.

Usually he was pretty talkative, but that night on our drive home he said very little. He didn't even mention going anywhere else; usually he asked if I wanted to have a hamburger or a pizza. In any case, I couldn't have swallowed anything.

It was very hot and sticky that night, but Kevin didn't even close the windows and turn on the air conditioning, as he usually did when it was really hot. He didn't draw me close to him, either. In fact, he didn't seem to notice me. And he started driving faster and faster.

"Kevin, please!" I said finally. "We're going too fast. If the state troopers come by, they'll stop you."

He looked at me as if seeing me for the first time in the past twenty minutes. "Sorry," he said. It seemed that he was making a conscious effort to be polite. "I didn't mean to scare you, Lisa. I was thinking of something else."

Meredith? I wanted to ask, but I didn't have the courage. What if he said yes? What if he said, "This is where you get off, Lisa"?

He did slow down a little, and I unclenched my hands, which I'd made into tight

93

little fists. The feeling of physical danger was past, but my spirits were so low, I couldn't think of anything lighthearted to say. Apparently Kevin couldn't either because when we got to my house, he gave me a quick little peck on the cheek and muttered, " 'Night, Lisa. See you soon." By the time I got to my front door, he was on his way.

I was just fitting my key into the lock when someone loomed up behind me, and I gave a little shriek. Then I realized it was Phil. "Where did you come from? You scared me out of my wits."

The porch light was on, and I could see that his face was white. He looked furious. I'd never seen Phil look like that, and I just stood still.

"You weren't half so scared as I was a little while ago. I was just coming back from the city when suddenly Kevin's car zoomed right past me. I could see that you were inside. I couldn't believe the way he was driving, so I followed along as fast as I dared, in case you both ended up in a ditch."

"I don't need a keeper, Phil! Kevin knows what he's doing. You don't have to worry about me—ever." I wouldn't have let him know, for a million dollars, how terrified I'd been as Kevin raced home from the Rock Inn.

Phil stared at me without a word. Then he

said coldly, "Sorry I interfered," and went off the porch two steps at a time.

I let myself into the house, climbed the stairs to my room, and cried for an hour.

Chapter Ten

When I went downstairs the next morning at eight, I could smell pancakes and sausage cooking on the griddle. From my father's little study came the sounds of his accordion. I went into our sunny kitchen, where my mother sat drinking coffee and reading the Sunday paper.

"He's starting early," I said to my mother.

"Well, you know your father. He's been up since six; this is the best part of the day to him. I'm glad there's plenty of space between us and the neighbors. Some of them might like to sleep late on Sunday morning." She studied me. "You look a little sleepy-eyed. I heard you come in."

Maybe she'd heard me yelling at Phil and wondered what was going on. But if I told her Kevin had been driving too fast and that Phil had been worried, she wouldn't have wanted me to date Kevin again, and I wouldn't have been able to stand that. *If* he asked me for another date, that was.

So I just said, "We had a pretty good time. We went to the Rock Inn, but it was awfully crowded and noisy." I got myself a glass of orange juice. "I'm not sure I'm hungry enough for pancakes, Mom."

"Sit," she ordered. "This is brunch. I'm not fixing lunch today, so you'd better eat now."

"Sure," I said, pouring maple syrup onto the pancakes Mom put before me.

"Here," my mother said, putting another pancake on my plate. "And have some sausages."

My appetite seemed to have come back, in spite of my worries. I packed away three pancakes with butter and real maple syrup, plus two sausages, and a glass of orange juice.

"That was great, Mom. I feel better now," I said.

She gave me one of her understanding looks, but she didn't ask any questions. She knew I'd tell her what was bothering me when

I was ready. She left the kitchen, and I heard her call to my father.

Stacking the dishes in the dishwasher and wiping off the round oak table, I found myself thinking of Kevin and his behavior the night before, and of Phil, who I knew must be pretty angry with me. But my thoughts were interrupted when the phone rang. In a moment my mother called, "Lisa? It's for you."

I went into the hallway and picked up the phone. "Lisa?" It was Phil's voice.

In a rush we both said what I'd been wanting to say all morning. "I'm sorry." Then we laughed a little. "I really do apologize, Phil," I added. "Kevin *was* driving too fast, but I didn't want you to think I needed anyone to look after me."

"That's OK. If I'd had any sense, I wouldn't have come up on your porch once I knew you were home safely. I was just so mad at Kevin. I wanted you to know how I felt before I came to work."

We talked for a few more minutes, and by the time we hung up, I felt much better. Phil was certainly a good friend, and he was easy to be with. His conversation wasn't so polished as Kevin's, but he was interesting, and his nature was as sunny as his hair.

Mom and Dad went off to Rochester for a day's outing, and when Phil arrived to pick me up, I was ready for work. Since it was still warm, I was wearing new white shorts and a blue- and white-striped T-shirt.

"You look nice, Lisa," he said.

I returned his smile. "So do you." And he did, in cutoff jeans and a navy T-shirt. His slightly wavy, blond hair flopped over his forehead, and his eyes were *so* blue. Kevin's features were more conventionally handsome, but I thought any girl would go for Phil, too. With a little pang, I thought of Betsy Farrell. Had Phil just dropped her off the night before when he spotted Kevin and me dashing down the road? Then I checked myself. *You don't want him,* I thought, *but you don't want anyone else to have him, either.*

I handed Phil a cardboard carton and said, "Handle this box carefully. It has fried chicken and rolls and potato salad. You know my mother. Even though she and Dad are going out to lunch, she was afraid you and I might starve."

He sniffed appreciatively. "Smells wonderful. I think your mother is great. Mine, too." He held up a big plastic bag filled with chocolate-chip cookies, Mrs. Bradley's specialty.

"Wow. Do you get the feeling our mothers think we need fattening up?"

"Whatever the reason," he said," we're the winners."

The store smelled a little musty from the heat and the old books, but we opened the windows and let in fresh air and sunshine. I put the chicken and salad in the refrigerator and poured glasses of iced tea, adding fresh mint from our garden. Phil lined up some books on the old school desk on the porch.

Phil and I seemed very compatible, both of us acting as though we wanted to make up for our fits of temper the night before. I know that I had a strong need to keep his friendship and I wasn't going to do anything to upset him.

The store got pretty busy that afternoon, and we had to postpone the fried chicken and salad for quite a while. One ruddy-cheeked man bought a whole armload of books, and two women, beautifully dressed, bought some fairly expensive antiques. A little blond girl, with her adoring parents, fell in love with a stuffed cat that Phil and I had bought at a garage sale. She loved it so much, I was tempted to give it to her, but Phil frowned at me.

"We're supposed to be making a success of this shop," he said after they'd left. But his smile was tender. "I think you and your father need a hardheaded businessman like me!"

He was right, of course. My father was

inclined to sell a book or antique at cost if a customer looked appreciative. And I, as my mother would say, was "cut from the same piece of cloth." Phil was flexible, but much more businesslike. We did need him.

When there was a lull, finally, we dug into the fried chicken and potato salad. Needless to say, the food was delicious. The air was nicer than it had been on Saturday, and we enjoyed the late-August breeze, which had a hint of early autumn in it.

"I hope we can keep this going," I said dreamily. "I do love it."

The phone rang, and I jumped. The telephone in the bookshop didn't get much use. Mostly it was there in case of emergencies. It was Kimberly. "I thought you might be there. I haven't heard from you in the past few days."

Instantly I felt guilty. "Sorry," I said feebly. "I've been pretty busy with Kevin the last few days."

She didn't make a joke as she normally would have done. I was beginning to sense reservation in her attitude toward Kevin. Probably it was because we hadn't double-dated with her and Steve. It might have hurt her feelings, and I couldn't blame her. No matter how many times I asked Kevin, he never wanted to double with anyone. After the funny way he'd acted the previous night, I wondered whether he'd deliberately been avoiding his friends and mine during the summer.

"Look, Lisa, Mrs. Kramer, the real estate lady, was here. She wanted to talk to your father, and she knows we're all friends, so she stopped at our house to find out where he was. I'm pretty sure she's on her way to the shop. Just thought I'd let you know."

"Thanks, Kimberly. Talk to you tonight, OK?"

Immediately I began to feel worried. Why would Mrs. Kramer want to talk to Dad, unless it was about someone who wanted to buy the shop? We'd had people looking at it, of course, but so far no one had been serious about it. Still, my father had made no promises to let me keep the store, he'd just said he'd give me a chance to run it for the summer. He might be forced to sell, especially if someone offered him a good price. I didn't *think* we'd lost money that summer, but I'd been too busy to tote up the exact expenses and sales. My bookkeeping had been very general.

Before I could tell Phil much about Kimberly's call, I heard someone come into the shop and knock on one of the wooden counters. I went into the main room, and there was Mrs. Kramer with a jolly-looking, balding man. Mrs. Kramer is short and square and noisy, and one of the best real estate people around. My heart sank when I saw the two of them together. They looked as if they meant business—real estate business.

Mrs. Kramer introduced us to Mr. Brunswick. "Mr. Brunswick is from Buffalo," she said proudly, as though she'd conjured him up all by herself. "He's tired of the corporate world, and he wants to have his own business in a small town." I couldn't think of what to say. I could see my dream going right down the tube. "Is your father here, Lisa?" Mrs. Kramer asked.

"He and Mom are in the city today," I said quickly.

"Well, that's all right. Mr. Brunswick can have a look around."

Watching miserably as she took him through the shop, I kept wishing that the place looked a mess, but it didn't. Everything was well dusted and in order. Phil and I had really been working on it these past weeks. The sunlight had laid a mellow glow on the old wooden tables and display cases. The books were arranged as if they were part of someone's private library. It looked like the kind of place a man like Mr. Brunswick, a man with a dream of his own, would want to run.

But this was my grandfather's store, I wanted to tell him. *And my father's. And I want it to be mine, someday at least.* But I couldn't say anything, so I left him to his happy browsing and went outside to join Phil on the porch.

He cast a look of sympathy at me. "Cheer up, it's not sold yet. And we've been doing pretty well this summer, so your father may decide to keep the store in the family for a while." He grinned at me. "I know you haven't been worrying about the money end, but I've been keeping track of sales and expenses, and you're ahead, Lisa, my girl."

Then he blushed as though he'd said something stupid, and I realized it was because he'd called me 'Lisa, my girl'—and I was Kevin's girl.

Impulsively, without thinking how it would sound, without asking myself why I was asking such a personal question, I asked, "Is Besty Farrell your girlfriend?"

For a minute I thought he wasn't going to answer me, then he said quietly, "No. Why would you think that? I've only dated her twice."

It struck me then that Phil and I had lost some of our old easiness together. It made me feel sad and sort of lonely.

As though he felt it, too, he said stiffly, "I know you're dating Kevin Cott, and I'm not trying to interfere, but would you like to go to the Strong Museum on Wednesday afternoon? I thought the collection of Victorian antiques and dolls they have might give us some ideas about what to buy at sales. And I can have my mom's car Wednesday, so we can be sure of transporation."

"I'd love it," I said and meant it. I'd been meaning to visit the museum for ages but hadn't gotten around to it.

Just then Mrs. Kramer and Mr. Brunswick came out on the porch. In her booming voice, Mrs. Kramer said, "Tell your father I must see him tomorrow sometime, Lisa, even if it's in the evening. Mr. Brunswick is quite taken with your shop." She bestowed a happy smile on Phil and me, then took off with her client.

Phil and I looked at each other, and I knew the dismay I saw on his face was reflected on my own. "Oh, Phil, oh, Phil," I said, and tears came streaming down my cheeks.

"Please don't cry, Lisa," he said, his voice sounding strange and muffled. "It'll work out all right."

He grabbed a great wad of tissues from a box on the windowsill and stuffed it into my hand. For just a second, I thought he was going to put his arms around me, but he didn't. He just let me cry until I couldn't cry any more.

I looked at him, knowing that my eyes

were puffy and red and that I must look terrible, but it didn't matter. "Thanks," I said. "I needed that."

"I know." His eyes were kind, but I saw something else there, something I didn't like very much. Pity. And I wasn't sure why.

Chapter Eleven

Saturday night's sinking feel about Kevin's deserting me carried on into Monday, too, a feeling made worse by my fear that my dad would sell the store. I knew I should be practical. He needed the money. But I loved that place too much to give it up without a fight.

Kimberly came by to visit for a couple of hours on Monday afternoon. My mother was working, and Phil had gone to a good sale in the city, so I had to stay on duty at the shop. Kimberly and I sat playing backgammon on the porch, waiting for customers.

"Mrs. Kramer is going to meet with my dad tonight," I said gloomily. "I know she wants to sell the store to that Mr. Brunswick.

She'll probably convince Dad that I'm too young to keep on running the place by myself." I added hastily, "Not really by myself, of course. Phil is great, and he's learning more about books and antiques all the time."

Kimberly took a long drink of iced tea and bit into one of Mrs. Bradleys' chocolate-chip cookies, then said in her practical way, "Well, you've done all right so far. Maybe your father won't sell."

"Maybe." All the time I'd been holding back the events of Saturday night, but I knew I'd end up telling Kimberly everything. We've been friends too long to have secrets. Sometimes she's very tough on me, when she thinks my flights of fancy are too wild, but she's also very understanding when something's really bothering me.

So I told her everything, including the part about Kevin's change of attitude after Sharon and Tony came along. Just by the careful way in which she said nothing, I knew that she wasn't surprised, that all along she'd considered my dating Kevin a summer fling for him.

"But he did say he hoped Meredith would invite him and me to her party! That's something, isn't it, Kimberly?"

"Sure," she said, her eyes on the backgammon board. "Don't worry, Lisa. He'll probably stop by sometime this week."

Phil pulled up in front of the store then, and the conversation became general. Kimberly went in and got a tall glass of iced tea for Phil, who was sweating from the sun. It made me mad, the way she obviously preferred Phil to Kevin, but Kimberly didn't change her mind easily, so I didn't even try anymore.

"They didn't have many reasonable antiques," Phil told us, gulping his tea and grabbing one of the last of his mother's cookies, "but I found some really neat books. Remember Mrs. Cooke, the lady who asked us to keep an eye out for old editions of Louisa May Alcott?"

Mrs. Cooke was eighty-six and bright as a new penny, and she collected old children's books. Every now and again my father found one for her collection, and she was always so pleased. "I remember those books from my childhood," she said. "When I'm gone, they'll go to the university. But right now, I just love to read them over and over again."

Phil put two of his finds on the table next to the backgammon set. A copy of *Jo's Boys* and one of *Little Women,* two Louisa May Alcott books. They were in beautiful condition, and they were very early editions.

111

"I'll call Mrs. Cooke tomorrow," I said. "She'll love these, Phil."

He looked pleased and kind of shy. I could hardly believe we'd been so hostile toward each other only a couple of nights before. I wanted to be friends with Phil, and it had hurt to have him act so coldly toward me. Sometimes I felt as though I'd known him all my life, instead of just months.

After a while some customers came. Kimberly got up and said, "I'd better get on home. I have to start dinner."

"Drive you home?" Phil offered.

"Thanks, but no thanks. It's not that far. I feel like walking."

After Kimberly and the customers had gone, Phil said, "Any word about the shop?"

I shook my head. "My parents have to see Mrs. Kramer tonight. Dad said he isn't making any decisions until he's heard her out."

An hour later I was dusting off a row of books at the back of the shop when a pair of hands grabbed my waist. I nearly fainted from the shock, but Kevin's soothing smile was more than enough to revive me—and my sagging spirits.

"I didn't mean to scare you," he said, noting my surprised expression. "I guess you didn't hear me come in. You ought to have a bell or something by the front door."

"Yes, I suppose," I said, surprised I could get any words out. I guess I'd already convinced myself I wouldn't be hearing from Kevin, not after the way he acted Saturday night. "What's up?"

"Hey, can't a guy come around and see his girl?" I must have beamed just then because he added, "That's more like the greeting I expected—though I suppose I don't deserve it. I wasn't exactly the world's best company the other night."

"That's not true," I protested. But to be honest, I didn't really hear what he said after the words "his girl." I felt so relieved. He did care about me. All my worrying had been for nothing.

Kevin shook his head. "I know how I acted. I got weird when Sharon mentioned Meredith. Kind of stupid isn't it? I hadn't thought about her in ages. Anyway, I thought I ought to come over and apologize—and see if you wanted to split a split with me at Polly's tonight."

"I wish I could, Kevin, but I'm not in the mood to go anywhere. They may have found a buyer for the shop. Dad's meeting with the real estate agent tonight."

"That's terrible," Kevin said. "After all the work you've put into the place."

"And Phil, too," I added, without thinking.

"Yeah." Kevin snorted. "Though how much of a help he could be, I can't figure out. Every time I come in here he's either hiding out back or he has his nose stuck in a book."

"You're not being fair," I said. At that moment Phil was in the back cataloging a new batch of books. "Why, I never could have gotten through the summer without him. He helped me rearrange the place and buy new merchandise and keep all the records. He—" I stopped abruptly, realizing how true it was and how absurd it was to be building him up in front of Kevin.

"He what?" Kevin wanted to know. His voice was full of restrained anger—or maybe even jealousy.

"He—he's been a valuable employee," I finished somewhat lamely. "And he won't even be that much longer if this buyer turns out to be for real."

Kevin rubbed his hands along my shoulders. "Maybe it'll all be for the best, Lisa. After all, school's going to start up again soon, and the last thing you'll need is a business to run."

"But I planned to keep working then, too. After school and on weekends."

"But what about activities and Saturday afternoon football games and stuff like that?" Kevin pulled away and walked over to the butter churn. From the way he talked, you would have thought I was a monk about to cloister myself for the next thousand years.

"I guess I'll miss out on some of that. But this shop is worth it. Besides," I added, "I never cared much for football, anyway."

I didn't like the way Kevin looked at me just then, like I'd thrown water in his face or stepped on his favorite record. Clearly what I'd said hadn't pleased him. But I'd meant it and couldn't take back the words even if I wanted to. In a way, though, I felt relieved to be so open with him.

"I guess football's not for everybody," he said, taking a few steps closer to the door. "It's no big deal. I've got to run now, but I'll see you this weekend, OK?"

It wasn't until much later that I realized he'd left without kissing me.

That evening, when Dad and Mom and Mrs. Kramer were in Dad's little study, I cleaned up the kitchen and finally went up to my room. It made me nervous to have them holed up in there so long. I had the feeling Mr. Brunswick, through Mrs. Kramer, had made Dad "an offer he couldn't refuse." That's the way

Mrs. Kramer talked, but I realized miserably that it might be true.

Finally I heard the front door close and knew that Mrs. Kramer had left. But I didn't want to go downstairs and find out what had happened. I was too scared.

About half an hour later Dad called up the stairs to me, and I went down, feeling as though all my nerve endings were exposed. He and Mom were both standing at the foot of the stairs, their faces very serious. The news couldn't be good.

"Come on in the study," Dad said. "So we can talk things over."

Mom brought in a pot of tea and three cups. Dad's study is very small, but it has a window seat and many bookshelves, plus an overflowing rolltop desk. Dad's old accordion lay on a chair, but I knew he wasn't going to play it that night.

I sat down and sipped some tea, but I couldn't eat the orange-coconut cookies Mom had made. Normally I can't keep my hands off them.

At last Dad said, his voice heavy, "You've probably guessed that Mr. Brunswick has made an offer for the shop. It's a good offer, Lisa, and Mrs. Kramer is pushing me to take it."

"Naturally," I said bitterly.

Mom gave me a sharp look. "Lisa, she's only doing her job."

"I don't see how you can cut away part of your life—and my life, too, just for money."

My father said, his voice sad, "I know. But we do have some heavy doctor's bills to catch up on. And your college is coming up in another year. That's the most important item."

"But Mom has a part-time job, and you have a job with a salary now. Couldn't we get by?"

He hesitated, then said, "I'll tell you what we'll do. You bring me all your figures for the store, and we'll go over our expenses and assets. Maybe we can swing it."

For a moment my heart sang, but then, just as quickly, it stopped. I'd been having too good a time all summer to keep any real accounts. I had some rough figures, but nothing detailed. Then I remember what Phil had said when he'd called me "Lisa, my girl."

I said boldly, "I think we're ahead, Dad. Phil has been keeping the accounts. I'll ask him for all the facts."

Mom raised her eyebrows a little at that. She's always been after Dad to be more businesslike, possibly to buy a small computer for bookkeeping.

"Well," she said briskly, "that takes care of

that for the moment. Now have some cookies, Lisa. You have a reprieve."

I laughed with relief. "Phil and I are going to the Strong Museum Wednesday, if you can stay in the shop for a few hours," I said.

"Of course. How nice!" She acted as though I'd said I was going somewhere with Matt Dillon or somebody. Sometimes she and Kimberly thought alike.

"It's mostly business," I offered coolly.

On Wednesday Mom went to the shop, and Phil picked me up at the house. It was raining, but the air was balmy and had a wonderful, wet, flowery fragrance.

"This may be a wasted trip, as far as business goes," I told Phil. "Mom and Dad haven't made up their minds yet, but if they sell the shop, obviously we won't need any more knowledge of the book or antique business."

Phil started up the car. "Well, it's my excuse for going to look at Mrs. Strong's collection of toys and books and furniture, and I'm not giving it up."

Margaret Woodbury Strong was a tremendously wealthy woman who had collected thousands and thousands of things, dolls and toys, china and books, furniture, anything that caught her fancy. When she died, she left sixty million dollars to establish a museum to

118

enable other people to enjoy her wonderful collections.

I hadn't been to the museum before, probably because, as Mom said, people tended to ignore the treasures right under their noses. The building was gray concrete and looked modern for a Victorian museum. I felt a pang of excitement as we parked the car and went inside.

There was so much to see, I knew one visit wasn't going to be enough. It took my breath away to see the nineteenth-century pottery and porcelain and silver, the furniture and household furnishings of middle-class life a hundred years ago.

Phil was taken by the mechanical toys, while I examined every detail of the beautiful dollhouses. "I'd love to have been a child then!" I said. "Imagine making up stories around some of these houses. You could live a whole, perfect life inside one of them."

We went on to the hundreds of dolls. "I must admit I can't identify too much with these," Phil said, grinning at me. "But it's pretty interesting to see the different kinds."

We laughed together at the bisque dolls from Germany because their painted faces were all the same—rosy cheeked, with pretty smiles. "It's like walking through a fairyland," I said as we strolled along, admiring the

119

wind-up toys and the peddler and fortune teller dolls. "And everything is arranged so beautifully."

Finally we had to leave, even though we'd covered only half the exhibits. I caught Phil's hand in mine, without thinking what I was doing. "It's given me a hundred ideas, Phil. Now I can see that the secret is in the way things are exhibited. I know the shop is teeny compared to all this, but we can display things better, show them off."

As we left the building and went to the parking lot, we were still hand in hand, our fingers laced loosely. The warmth of Phil's hand against mine felt good, comfortable. For a moment I wondered whether I had grabbed his hand out of friendship or because I was imagining I was sharing this moment with Kevin. Certainly I wished I had been there with Kevin, although I knew the Strong Museum wasn't really his type of place.

I turned to business, a safe but important topic. "Phil, thank you for taking me. Now I'm more determined than ever to keep the store running, if only my parents will let us keep it. Dad wants facts and figures for this summer. I told him you'd kept track of things. Could you come over tonight and show him we've been making a profit?"

He gave me a funny little grin. "You sure

know how to make a guy feel good. Yeah, I'll be over."

After that we drove slowly home in the rain, and for the time being, I felt contented instead of worried.

Chapter Twelve

I didn't hear from Kevin again until Friday, and then he stopped at the bookshop just before I closed up. Phil was still there, but he stayed in the back—just as he had the other day. It occurred to me then that Kevin had been right; Phil always avoided him as much as possible. I knew it was because he was jealous.

"Want to go in to Bragdon for a hamburger or pizza?" Kevin asked as he wandered restlessly around the store. He touched some of the antiques out on display but acted as though he didn't really see them.

"Yes, but I'll have to stop off and tell my mother, or she'll wait dinner." I looked doubtfully at my shorts and T-shirt. "Maybe I should change. I'm not exactly dressed for going out."

"You look fine. We'll go someplace simple."

I yelled to Phil that I was closing up, and he came out, said a quick hello to Kevin, then left.

I locked the store and got in Kevin's car. We were at my house in about two minutes, it seemed. "Want to come in?" I asked.

He was lounging against the seat, the motor still running. "No, I'll wait, thanks."

When I was with Kevin, I always seemed to be hurrying, and I did that now, running in to the kitchen to tell Mom I was going to eat out, kissing Dad, who was watching the evening news in the living room, rushing into the bathroom to comb my hair and put on fresh makeup. *Maybe,* I thought, *it's because I'm unsure of myself that I try so hard to do things the way Kevin wants them done. If I were like Meredith, I'd be cool and take it for granted that things would be done at my pace. Fat chance,* I thought and ran out to the car again.

We went to Polly's Sweet Shoppe and ordered hamburgers and Cokes. Looking around, I didn't see anyone we knew. The crowd was older at that hour. We ate and talked, mostly about school, which would soon be open.

"Have you talked your father into keeping the store?"

I shrugged. "Mrs. Kramer got him a good offer, but he hasn't made up his mind yet. Phil took over the receipts the other night. We made a profit, which is a point in our favor."

He smiled like the old, charming Kevin again. "I'll keep my fingers crossed for you. Actually, I wish there was something I wanted to do as much as you want to run that shop." He scowled. "I'll probably become a top-level businessman, like my father, and make lots of money, also like my father. Bor-ing."

We each had a dish of Polly's wonderful soft ice cream, and when we were finished, he said casually, "Meredith called me. Tomorrow night she and her brother Jerry are giving a party for Neil Hennessey, Jerry's roommate. They're going to have Freddy Fontaine there."

"Live?" I asked, forgetting to sound blasé about it.

Kevin laughed. "That's the best way," he said, teasing.

"That's class," I admitted.

Freddy Fontaine was a popular disc jockey from Rochester, and I'd heard he could be hired to run private parties. But I could imagine the look I'd get from my parents if I suggested I'd like to hire Freddy Fontaine for a party.

"Meredith invited me to come and bring a date. Would you like to go?"

My heart jumped into my throat, but I tried to sound nonchalant. "Are you sure you want to take me? After all, you and Meredith went together for a long time. It might be embarrassing."

Once again he gave me that charming smile. "Of course I want you to go with me. Pick you up at eight, OK?"

"OK." I wasn't sure it would be OK, but I did want to go.

After that we drove around for a while, then went back to my house and sat out in the backyard. The days were getting shorter already, and it was almost dark. We sat on the old wicker sofa and held hands. Once in a while Kevin would lean over and kiss me. I forgot all my anxieties, all my doubts, and just closed my eyes, listening to the crickets chirping.

I tried not to think of the next night because I was feeling pretty nervous about attending a party at Meredith's house. Instead, I just let myself enjoy the moment. It was so nice to have Kevin relaxed and loving, and not dashing off somewhere. I liked to take time to dream a little.

"It's nice here," he said. He kissed me again, very softly. "You're nice, Lisa." It wasn't exactly *I love you, Lisa*, but it made me feel pretty good, anyway.

I was disappointed when he didn't stay too long, but at least he gave me one more wonderful kiss and said, "See you tomorrow night."

Saturday seemed to last forever, but I got through it somehow, mostly because we were pretty busy. Phil and I went to a couple of garage sales in the morning, while Dad minded the store. In the afternoon we had a lot of customers because it was a beautiful late-summer day and people were out taking country drives. Phil and I were kept hopping practically every minute, and sales were really good.

I had the feeling Phil wanted to say something to me, something I didn't want to hear, so I kept bustling around. If he asked me for a date that night, I'd have to refuse, and I liked him too much to hurt his feelings. Better he didn't ask at all.

When it was nearly time to go home, I said quickly, not looking at him too closely, "Would you mind locking up, Phil? I'm going out later, and I want to get ready."

"I'll take care of it," he said, although he didn't sound too happy about it.

As I walked to my house, I was perspiring heavily and I knew I was really scared about the evening before me. I didn't think I was going to have much fun as a guest in Meredith Hunt's house.

With Mom frowning at me a little, I rushed through dinner, just pretending to enjoy the chicken casserole, which I usually loved. I didn't even question Dad about the possible bookshop sale.

My shower and shampoo relaxed me a little. When I put on my makeup, I used more than I usually did. After much thought, I'd decided to wear my black dress again. It was by far the most sophisticated thing I owned, and I knew it would take a lot to measure up to the standards of Meredith and Sharon and their friends. I added a couple of gold chains and matching earrings and decided I could hold my own.

Kevin was late, and as the minutes ticked away, I began to panic. Had he changed his mind and decided not to take me? Time crawled by. I kept looking in the mirror, afraid that I really looked like something out of a horror novel instead of a reasonably attractive, blond-haired girl. The trouble was. I wasn't Meredith Hunt and never would be. *Be quiet,*

Lisa, I said silently to my reflection in the mirror. *He's liked you well enough to date you all this summer. You're not a freak, you know.*

Then, sounding like cathedral bells, the doorbell rang. Kevin! I put on a little more lip gloss, to replace what I'd licked off in my anxiety. Mom called to me, and I went downstairs, trying to appear cool and collected.

"You look better every time I see you," Kevin said.

"Thanks." I smiled.

We said goodbye to my parents and went out into the Lincoln. The Hunts lived on the outskirts of Bragdon. If such a small town could be said to have a suburb, that's where Meredith lived. While most of the houses in Kingsway and Bragdon were old-fashioned Victorian and gingerbread houses, Meredith's house was modern, wide and sprawling, situated on about two acres of land. They had a pool and a sauna, and a corral for Meredith's horse. I'd never been there before, but I'd had it pointed out to me.

"Well, here goes," Kevin said as he rang the bell. He looked as confident as ever, but I had a feeling he was a little uncomfortable. After all, he'd always been there as Meredith's date, and now he had a different girl with him.

I was relieved when Jerry Hunt, Mere-

129

dith's brother, answered the door. Jerry was tall and good-looking and friendly, and he smiled at me warmly when Kevin introduced me. "Come on in, the party's under way."

As soon as we got inside, I could hear Freddy Fontaine's voice over the mike as he introduced a song. Then the music crashed into the room, pounding away. My own heart seemed to be pounding almost as loudly.

There were couples sprawled on chairs and sofas in the huge living room, and on the big screened sun porch, lots of couples were dancing. A number of the people looked older; Jerry's friends, I assumed.

"Want to dance?" Kevin asked.

"Love to." I remembered what my mother had always told me and held myself tall. If I couldn't be petite, I might just as well make the most of my five feet, eight inches—plus heels. At least I stood out a crowd. I decided to enjoy myself and forget about Meredith. Kevin and I swung onto the crowded floor and began to dance. Lots of people greeted him, and he introduced me to the ones I didn't know. There were a few knowing grins from some of the boys. I knew these were unspoken comments on the big breakup between Kevin and Meredith, but I tried not to care. Most of the girls seemed friendly enough, except Sharon, who darted a glance at us, then looked away again.

Eventually, of course, we had to greet our hostess. Arm in arm with a tall blond guy, she came in from the garden and made straight for Kevin and me. She wore a white dress with very narrow shoulder straps, and it set off her perfect tan wonderfully. Her long, wavy, dark hair was pinned up in a glamorous hairstyle, and she looked absolutely, stunningly beautiful. My heart began to thump so loudly I was afraid she could hear it.

"Well, hi, you two," she said. "This is Neil Hennessey. Lisa Randall and Kevin Cott." Her huge dark eyes flashed a triumphant look at Kevin as though to say, "Look at your replacement!"

I thought Neil was nice, but too grown-up for a sixteen-year-old girl, even one as mature as Meredith. But he seemed to admire her. Meredith didn't really say much to me. I could tell from the way she looked at me that she didn't think a lot of me. She talked on and on to Kevin about all the places they'd been in Europe.

"We'd better mingle," she said to Neil after a few minutes. She threw us a gorgeous smile, "Help yourselves to punch and food in the dining room. See you later."

They left, wending their way through the

crowd. Kevin and I went on dancing. He seemed perfectly composed, and that made me feel a little better, although I decided I'd never be really comfortable around Meredith.

"Meredith looks beautiful," I managed to say.

"Yeah. She's a pretty girl," Kevin said casually.

We danced, talked about school starting, and threw comments back and forth with the other kids. Everything seemed anticlimactic after our chat with Meredith and Neil, and I had a feeling she'd meant it to be that way. But what about Kevin? Did he have that same feeling of being let down, as though the excitement of the party had already peaked? I thought he might because he was awfully quiet, and usually Kevin was very lively, full of laughter and jokes.

We danced without talking, and pretty soon he said, "Want to go have something to drink or eat?"

"Love it," I answered. "I'm dying of thirst."

The dining room furnishings would have made my father's mouth water. The living room was decorated with modern furniture, but the dining room had an antique mahogany table and chairs, probably family heirlooms, a fruitwood buffet, and a mahogany and glass china cabinet. In the cabinet were

132

delicately worked silver platters and china plates. They were all beautiful, and I found myself thinking how much Phil would like these things, too.

We served ourselves all kinds of Chinese food and soda. It was delicious, of course. Meredith had gotten a fantastic Chinese restaurant to do the catering. We took our plates into the living room, sat on a comfortable couch, and talked with Kevin's friends. I was having a good time, but it wasn't really my kind of fun. I liked small parties where I knew everyone. *If only Kimberly and Steve and Phil were here*, I thought. I needed them that night, needed someone on my side. Not that Kevin *wasn't* on my side. But he belonged here and I didn't. It made me see how different from each other we really were.

At that moment, as if to show me how wrong I was, he put his arm around my shoulder and said, "Having fun?" His smile was so warm, his arm so comforting, that my mood brightened.

"Wonderful. Thanks for bringing me."

He kissed me then, a little light kiss, and I melted against him. He did like me!

Then I looked up, and there, standing in the doorway leading to the sun porch, were Meredith and Neil. She was looking straight at us. There was a sneering smile on her mouth, and her eyes shot sparks.

I looked at Kevin, and I knew then that his kiss and caress hadn't really been for me. They'd been for Meredith. He wanted to show her that he wasn't jealous of Neil, that he'd also found someone new.

Chapter Thirteen

On the way home Kevin was so sweet and attentive that I wondered if I'd imagined his reason for kissing me at the party. For one thing, he drove carefully, and I knew he was doing that for me. There was practically no traffic, and as we rode along, he kept one hand on mine on the seat. In the dark, I closed my eyes, savoring the warmth of his strong fingers. How I hated the summer to end! It had been magical, full of love and excitement, and I knew there could never be another like it.

When we got to my house, Kevin turned off the engine and drew me into his arms. "What are you dreaming about, Lisa?" he asked, his voice low and gentle. "You're so quiet."

"Oh—everything. The party, school, the bookshop."

He leaned over and kissed me, his lips so warm and soft that I thought I was in heaven. This certainly wasn't a kiss meant for Meredith. He liked *me*, Lisa Randall! I snuggled against his shoulder for a while, feeling so much happier.

"Did you hear some of the kids are planning an old-fashioned hayride for next week?" he said. "One more fling before school starts. The whole class will go, I guess, if they can contact everyone by telephone. Would you like to go with me? It's not just couples, more of a group thing, but I'd like to take you."

"Yes, yes, yes," I murmured, my lips against his throat.

We sat there for quite a while, and when he finally left, I floated into the house, my whole mood restored to happiness. Usually I read before I fell asleep, but that night I just got ready for bed and turned off the light. The moonlight drifted in the window, wrapping me in its romantic light.

Kimberly stopped by the shop on Monday so that I could fill her in on the party. She also mentioned the hayride. "You're going, aren't you, Phil?" she asked when he came out on the porch with an armload of old books.

I saw the tiny glance he gave me before he said, "I think so. It sounds like fun. You don't go on hayrides in Brooklyn Heights. Steve told me it's going to be a group party for the whole class."

"Right." Kimberly looked as though she wanted to say more, but she didn't.

The rest of the week went by fairly quickly with one daytime visit from Kevin. Dad toiled over the accounts and figures each evening. Still no word from him. Phil and I redid some of the displays. The new arrangements looked good, although they were nothing, of course, compared to those at the museum. Phil was clever at lighting some of the dolls and other antiques, which sat on low shelves; they looked really beautiful.

"I can't bear to give it up, Phil," I said, my eyes misting as I looked around the big room. "I know it's stupid to be so attached to *things*, but this place is more than a bookshop to me."

His voice was quiet. "I know. You can feel the history in an old building like this, feel the presence of all the people who lived here. I hope someday I can write a novel about a place like this. The books and antiques seem to have a life of their own, don't they?"

I nodded, unable to speak. Phil and I understood each other, there was no denying that. It felt a little weird, knowing that he could read my mind and I his. That's how I knew when he wanted to ask me for a date or when I was hurting him. And I knew he'd feel very bad when he saw me with Kevin on the hayride.

But nothing could stop me from happily anticipating the ride on Saturday night. I wondered if Phil would take Betsy Farrell, but I didn't dare ask him. Phil and I could talk about just about anything—except our dates.

On Saturday night I dressed in what I thought would be a proper hayride costume, jeans, plaid shirt, and a cowboy hat of Dad's. No heavy makeup for this party, I decided, and contented myself with eye shadow and lip gloss.

We were supposed to meet at the school at nine o'clock. By then it would be dark enough for our moonlight ride. Kevin came about a quarter to nine, and we went zooming off in his parents' Lincoln.

"When you think of it," I said to him, "it seems silly to travel by car in order to ride in a wagon drawn by horses!"

Actually it was more than one wagon, since nearly everyone in our class was going. The horses were drawn up on a side road near the school, and we could hear them snorting and stomping in the early-September night.

There was a full moon, and that made everything seem more mysterious and exciting.

We climbed into one of the huge, crowded wooden wagons and found ourselves a little nest in the hay. It was surprising how many people that big old wagon held, and there were two other rigs besides. The hay, freshly mown, smelled sweet and clean, like a field in autumn. At the far end of the wagon, Scott Hillman was playing his guitar and singing softly. The atmosphere was charged with excitement. "It's the full moon," my father would have said, but I liked to think it was something magical.

With the *clip-clop* of the horses' shoes and the sounds of the guitar and my classmates' voices ringing in the air, I felt as though I were being transported back to an earlier time, to the days when our bookshop had been someone's farmhouse and horses had been the common mode of transportation.

"I do love it, don't you?" I asked Kevin.

"It's great," he said, giving my hand a little squeeze.

Now that we had left the street lamps of Bragdon behind, it seemed almost as clear as day. The full moon lit up the crowded wagon, and I could see everyone in great detail. Kimberly and Steve were in the wagon behind us, and they waved their arms and shouted at us. I saw Phil at the other end of our wagon with a group of kids, singing along with Scott's guitar. I didn't see Betsy with him.

Then, to my horror, I realized that Meredith was cuddled in the straw, almost next to us, her pretty face close to Jim Matheson's. Jim was one of the most popular boys in school, almost as popular as Kevin, but then, Meredith would never settle for anyone less. I knew that Jerry and Neil had gone back to college, and it hadn't taken her any time to find a substitute for Neil.

Kevin had seen Meredith and Jim at the same time I had. I could tell because I felt his body stiffen next to mine. But casual as usual, he just called, "Hi, Meredith, hi, Jim. That was a great party last week, Meredith. Jerry and Neil back at school?"

She smiled at him so sweetly. "Yes, back to the grind, isn't it awful?"

"Hey, Meredith," Jim said, "I'm going to go put in a request with Scott. I'll be right back." He went crawling down to the other end of the wagon, swaying with the action of the big wooden rig and leaving Kevin in between me and Meredith.

Just as if I weren't even there, Meredith patted the straw beside her. "Come on over for a minute, Kevin, so I can tell you more about Europe. It was so wonderful."

"You don't mind, do you, Lisa?"

What could I say? "No," I muttered.

Quickly he crawled over and settled down beside her—and I felt as if I would die right there. In less than a minute I had changed from a desirable, happy, sixteen-year-old girl to a rejected, miserable misfit. Smiling brightly, but stiffly, acting as if I didn't care, I leaned back against the straw and pretended to listen to the music. If Meredith hadn't been there, I would have cried, but I knew she'd see me, so I held my breath and smiled and smiled and smiled.

Then I became aware of someone moving toward me, weaving around the huddled couples, then settling down beside me. Phil! "Hi, Lisa. Did you hear my mellow voice singing those songs?" he asked. "The gentle braying of Phil Bradley?"

He kept talking like that, fooling around and being silly. It wasn't the way Phil usually talked. I wanted to put my arms around him and thank him because I knew he was saving me, protecting me from feeling hurt and humiliated.

We talked together for what seemed like ages, but I was agonizingly aware of Kevin and Meredith. They sat close together, murmuring in each other's ears and completely ignoring us. All around them, voices were laughing and screaming, but they were in a world of their own. To me, the sounds were deafening, and my head began to ache. If only Phil and I could slip off the wagon and go home! But that was impossible, so I let Phil go on talking, and I did my best to answer him.

Finally Jim worked his way back to Meredith. Obviously he and Meredith weren't serious about each other because he didn't seem to mind the fact that Kevin was with her. In fact, they all talked together for a few minutes.

Kevin did have good manners. He came back to me finally. Under his breath, Phil asked, "Want me to stay?"

I squeezed his hand. "I'll be OK. Thanks, Phil."

"Sorry, Lisa," Kevin said, looking a little self-conscious. "Meredith wanted to fill me in on her trip."

Since she had told everybody in sight about her trip at her homecoming party, I didn't think there could have been much more to tell, but I nodded, pretending to believe him.

I guess I knew it was all over then. Kevin and I didn't have much to say to each other during the rest of the ride to Johnston's Cider Mill. I gritted my teeth, knowing I had to stick it out for a few more hours. The cider mill was about twenty miles from Kingsway, and I had no way to get back home until the wagons took us.

I might hate the smell of sweet cider for the rest of my life. Normally I would have loved the sight of the long, barn-red building, in which fruits and vegetables were sold in daytime. That night baskets of apples and doughnuts and paper cups of sweet cider were lined up. There were lanterns and candles everywhere. It looked beautiful, but I couldn't enjoy it.

Kevin spent most of the time kidding around with his friends—and Meredith. Every now and then he'd come back and see how I was doing, but I knew his heart wasn't in it.

"Forget him, Lisa!" Kimberly told me. "The other day at the shop, I felt like telling you to come on the hayride with Phil. Meredith's back, and she knows exactly how to get Kevin back."

"I know," I said drearily. I couldn't get mad at Kimberly for being honest. I knew she was truly my friend and that she was hurting for me.

Somehow Phil managed to hover around, too, even when Kevin was with me, and that did make me feel a little better. Phil and Kimberly were my real friends, even though I had put them in the background all summer long.

At last, after what seemed like years, the wagons began loading up again for the trip back to Bragdon. Kevin sat with me, but he didn't put his arm around my shoulders. We rode back in the moonlight like two strangers, not the boy and girl in love I had believed us to be.

From the glances Kevin was giving Meredith on the way back, I knew he was going to run to her as soon as the wagon stopped. But I was wrong; he was too much of a gentleman to dump me so unceremoniously. When we climbed down from the haywagon, he took my hand for the first time in hours and led me to the big Lincoln. I wanted to stop and tell him I'd find another way to get back to Kingsway, but I had too much pride for that.

We sat in silence, each of us caught up in our own thoughts. When Kevin finally drove up to my house, I think we both felt relieved. "You don't have to walk me to the door," I told him as I reached for the door handle. Summoning up my courage I said, "We both know what happened tonight. You're going to start dating Meredith again."

Kevin didn't deny it, and I felt my heart break a little more. "I'm sorry Lisa," he whispered.

"I suppose it was inevitable," I said, trying to sound cheerful, though tears were starting

144

to blur my vision. "I mean how much longer could you stand to hang around someone who's always got her nose buried in a book? Besides, Meredith loves football."

Kevin reached for my hand, and I surprised myself by pulling away.

"Hey, Lisa. You really are special. I had a wonderful time with you this summer."

Sure, as a summer replacement for the girl you really love, I wanted to say. But Kevin did sound sincere, and I had no right to be bitter. Someday, after the hurt disappeared, I knew I'd realize that we really didn't have enough in common to keep the relationship going. Meredith's return only speeded up the process.

Then, almost under his breath, Kevin muttered, "Phil's going to be some lucky guy."

"Phil? What does he have to do with anything?"

Kevin gave me one of those grins that had made him so appealing to me. "I don't need to tell you what you already know. Good night, Lisa." Leaning over the seat, he kissed me gently on the cheek for the very last time.

Chapter Fourteen

"Did you have a good time last night?" my mother asked when I went into the kitchen Sunday morning.

"It was OK." I turned away from her and poured myself a cup of tea from the pot she had just brewed.

"Doesn't sound as though you had a really wonderful evening." She was busy turning a beautifully browned ham omelet.

Sooner or later, when I could talk about it without crying, I'd tell her that Kevin and I weren't going to see each other anymore.

"I'm not hungry," I said. "I'll go on down to the shop today if you and Dad want to do something together."

"Have some juice," she said. She knew something was wrong, but all she could do for me right then was urge some nutrition on me.

"I'm OK, Mom," I said and hugged her briefly. "See you later. Say goodbye to Dad." I knew he must be out in the garden by now, weeding and watering, as he loved to do.

Walking as fast as I could, I hurried down the tree-lined streets to Randall's Bookstore and Antique Shop. I saw two people strolling along and a few children playing on the Atwaters' big, sunny lawn. These were the same quiet streets I'd walked on all my life, yet that day I was different. The Lisa Randall in love with a dream had vanished.

As I approached the shop, I saw a tall, blond boy waiting on the sunny front steps, his head resting against the wooden post. It was Phil, tanned and good-looking in his white knit shirt and faded blue jeans. I went up and sat down beside him.

"Thanks for being so nice last night, Phil."

He turned his head and smiled. "I'd do anything for you, Lisa, you know that."

"I know." It was soothing that there was someone in the world, besides my parents, of course, who could be counted on.

The store started getting busy right after that, so Phil and I didn't have much chance to talk. I kept occupied and tried not to think about the night before, but it wasn't easy. Partly, I was angry at myself. I couldn't really be mad at Kevin. I truly felt he had liked and been attracted to me, although I now knew I'd been only a summer romance to him. Despite their quarrels, Meredith was the girl he truly loved.

Slowly the truth of this filtered in on my consciousness. Love can be so painful. It can start blissfully, but will always end painfully when there's no love on both sides. That was the way it was with Kevin and me.

I'd thought my parents were going in to the city, but to my surprise, they turned up at the shop that afternoon with refreshments. They brought chicken and rolls, a plate of fresh vegetables, and watermelon.

"Wow!" Phil said. "What a job this is! Books and home-cooked food."

To my surprise, I was starving, and I guessed that meant my heart wasn't completely broken. Mom made a pot of her favorite Twining's tea, and we all sat around the old table in the kitchen, eating and drinking and keeping an ear out for customers at the front of the shop. The sun shone in on the shabby old kitchen and made it look beautiful.

Finally Mom opened the big cake box she'd put up on the counter before we began

149

to eat. The box came from Molly's Bakery, and since it wasn't anyone's birthday, I was a little surprised. Mom didn't buy cakes too often. She thought fruit was a much more sensible dessert. But that day she took out a beautiful glazed chocolate cake, my favorite kind, and set it carefully on a plate, then brought it over to the table.

"Read it," she said with a big smile.

I looked at the delicate pink script on the glazed chocolate top. It said: Lisa Randall: Books, Inc. And below it, in smaller letters: Owner and Prop.

"Oh, Mom, Dad!" I screamed. "You mean you're not selling it?"

"I talked to Mrs. Kramer last night," Dad said. "I told her we couldn't let the shop go out of the family, so it's yours, honey."

I hugged him and Mom. And then, without thinking twice about it, I hugged Phil. His face turned scarlet, but he hugged me back, and I knew he was happy for me.

"Does this mean I still have a job?" A little smile was turning up the corners of his mouth, and I could see he felt good.

"Sure. It will have to be weekends once school starts," I told him. "And we can take turns opening the store for a couple of hours after school, at least while the weather's good and there's tourist traffic."

After Mom and Dad had left, Phil and I began to plan more improvements for the store, and we decided on our working hours. It was so exciting. I don't know why, but I felt like a new person. All summer I'd been so tense, so eager to please Kevin and to live up to his idea of what a girl should be that I'd forgotten how to relax.

Later, I sat cross-legged on the floor and looked over the new box of children's books Phil had bought at a garage sale. I didn't even care that my jeans were dusty and my nose smudged. That day I didn't have to keep myself in perfect order because I knew Kevin wouldn't be coming in anymore.

Phil wandered in from the front porch just then. "Find something you like?"

I looked up at him, smiling. "Did you ever read *A Bear Called Paddington* when you were little?" I asked him.

His grin was just like a little boy's. "It was my favorite. Before I could read, I had my mother read it to me over and over again. Later, I kept reading the book wishing I could go to Paddington Station in London and run into that bear."

I looked up, laughing. "Me, too," I said. "Last Christmas Kimberly gave me a big Paddington Bear, with real Wellington boots that you can take off. She knows how much I love him." I nodded down at the book I was reading. "This is a first edition. Don't you love the illustrations?"

He bent over to look at the pictures, then he looked at me, and for a minute I thought he was going to kiss me, but he didn't. What he said, though, was like a caress. "That's why you're so special to me, Lisa. You get so excited about little things."

It was my turn to blush. I didn't know why, but I could feel the blood rushing up to the roots of my hair. I bent my head over the book and wished I were Rapunzel, so that I could hide behind my long, golden hair.

He said softly, "It seems to me that two people who love Paddington Bear must have quite a lot in common."

I still didn't look at him. "I think you're right, Phil."

I wanted to tell him that I wasn't completely over the hurt Kevin had dealt me, but that I knew I was going to recover. I wanted to tell him that I understood real love is based on friendship, or it isn't real at all. I wanted him to know that I realized I'd hurt him. I wanted to say so much. But I didn't have to.

He reached out and took my hand in his. I looked up at him, and I knew that, even without words, he understood what I wanted to say.

A LETTER TO THE READER

Dear Friend,

Ever since I created the series, SWEET VALLEY HIGH, I've been thinking about a love trilogy, a miniseries revolving around one very special girl, a character similar in some ways to Jessica Wakefield, but even more devastating—more beautiful, more charming, and much more devious.

Her name is Caitlin Ryan, and with her long black hair, her magnificent blue eyes and ivory complexion, she's the most popular girl at the exclusive boarding school she attends in Virginia. On the surface her life seems perfect. She has it all: great wealth, talent, intelligence, and the dazzle to charm every boy in the school. But deep inside there's a secret need that haunts her life.

Caitlin's mother died in childbirth, and her father abandoned her immediately after she was born. At least that's the lie she has been told by her enormously rich grandmother, the cold and powerful matriarch who has raised Caitlin and given her everything money can buy. But not love.

Caitlin dances from boy to boy, never staying long, often breaking hearts, yet she's so sparkling and delightful that everyone forgives her. No one can resist her.

No one that is, but Jed Michaels. He's the new boy in school—tall, wonderfully handsome, and very, very nice. And Caitlin means to have him.

But somehow the old tricks don't work; she can't

seem to manipulate him. Impossible! There has never been anyone that the beautiful and terrible Caitlin couldn't have. And now she wants Jed Michaels—no matter who gets hurt or what she has to do to get him.

So many of you follow my SWEET VALLEY HIGH series that I know you'll find it fascinating to read what happens when love comes into the life of this spoiled and selfish beauty—the indomitable Caitlin Ryan.

Thanks for being there, and keep reading,

Francine Pascal

A special preview of the exciting
opening chapter of the first book
in the fabulous new trilogy:

CAITLIN

BOOK ONE

LOVING

---

by Francine Pascal,
creator of the best-selling
SWEET VALLEY HIGH series

"That's not a bad idea, Tenny," Caitlin said as she reached for a book from her locker. "Actually, it's pretty good."

"You really like it?" Tenny Sears hung on every word the beautiful Caitlin Ryan said. It was the petite freshman's dream to be accepted into the elite group the tall, dark-haired junior led at Highgate Academy. She was ready to do anything to belong.

Caitlin looked around and noticed the group of five girls who had begun to walk their way, and she lowered her voice conspiratorially. "Let me think it over, and I'll get back to you later. Meanwhile let's just keep it between us, okay?"

"Absolutely." Tenny struggled to keep her excitement down to a whisper. The most important girl in the whole school liked her idea. "Cross my heart," she promised. "I won't breathe a word to anyone."

Tenny would have loved to continue the conversation, but at just that moment Caitlin remembered she'd left her gold pen in French class. Tenny was only too happy to race to fetch it.

The minute the younger girl was out of sight, Caitlin gathered the other girls around her.

"Hey, you guys, I just had a great idea for this year's benefit night. Want to hear it?"

Of course they wanted to hear what she had to say about the benefit, the profits of which would go to the scholarship fund for miners' children. Everyone was always interested in anything Caitlin Ryan had to say. She waited until all eyes were on her, then hesitated for an instant, increasing the dramatic impact of her words.

"How about a male beauty contest?"

"A what?" Morgan Conway exclaimed.

"A male beauty contest," Caitlin answered, completely unruffled. "With all the guys dressing up in crazy outfits. It'd be a sellout!"

Most of the girls looked at Caitlin as if she'd suddenly gone crazy, but Dorothy Raite, a sleek, blond newcomer to Highgate, stepped closer to Caitlin's locker. "I think it's a great idea!"

"Thanks, Dorothy," Caitlin said, smiling modestly.

"I don't know." Morgan was doubtful. "How are you going to get the guys to go along with this? I can't quite picture Roger Wake parading around on stage in a swimsuit."

"He'll be the first contestant to sign up when I get done talking to him." Caitlin's tone was slyly smug.

"And all the other guys?"

"They'll follow along." Caitlin placed the last of her books in her knapsack, zipped it shut, then gracefully slung it over her shoulder. "Everybody who's anybody in this school will just shrivel up and die if they can't be part of it. Believe me, I wouldn't let the student council down. After all, I've got my new presidency to live up to."

Morgan frowned. "I suppose." She took a chocolate bar out of her brown leather shoulder bag and began to unwrap it.

Just at that moment, Tenny came back, empty-handed and full of apologies. "Sorry, Caitlin, I asked all over, but nobody's seen it."

"That's okay. I think I left it in my room, anyway."

"Did you lose something?" Kim Verdi asked, but Caitlin dismissed the subject, saying it wasn't important.

For an instant Tenny was confused until Dorothy Raite asked her if she'd heard Caitlin's fabulous new idea for a male beauty contest. Then everything fell into place. Caitlin had sent her away in order to take credit for the idea.

It didn't even take three seconds for Tenny to make up her mind about what to do. "Sounds terrific," she said. Tenny Sears was determined to belong to this group, no matter what.

Dorothy leaned over and whispered to Caitlin. "Speaking of beauties, look who's walking over here."

Casually Caitlin glanced up at the approaching Highgate soccer star. Roger Wake's handsome face broke into a smile when he saw her. Caitlin knew he was interested in her, and up until then she'd offhandedly played with that interest—when she was in the mood.

"And look who's with him!" Dorothy's elbow nearly poked a hole in Caitlin's ribs. "Jed Michaels. Oh, my God, I've been absolutely dying to meet this guy."

Caitlin nodded, her eyes narrowing. She'd been anxious to meet Jed, too, but she didn't tell Dorothy that. Ever since his arrival as a transfer student at Highgate, Caitlin had been studying him, waiting for precisely the right moment to be introduced and to make an unforgettable impression on him. It seemed that the opportunity had just been handed to her.

"Hey, Caitlin. How're you doing?" Roger called out, completely ignoring the other girls in the group.

"Great, Roger. How about you?" Caitlin's smile couldn't have been wider. "Thought you'd be on the soccer field by now."

"I'm on my way. The coach pushed back practice half an hour today, anyway. Speaking of which, I don't remember seeing you at the last scrimmage." There was a hint of teasing in his voice.

Caitlin looked puzzled and touched her fingertips to her lips. "I was there, I'm sure—"

"We were late, Caitlin, remember?" Tenny spoke up eagerly. "I was with you at drama club, and it ran over."

"Now, how could I have forgotten? You see,

Roger"—Caitlin sent him a sly, laughing look—"we never let the team down. Jenny should know—she's one of your biggest fans."

"Tenny," the girl corrected meekly. But she was glowing from having been singled out for attention by Caitlin.

"Oh, right, Tenny. Sorry, but I'm really bad with names sometimes." Caitlin smiled at the girl with seeming sincerity, but her attention returned quickly to the two boys standing nearby.

"Caitlin," Dorothy burst in, "do you want to tell him—"

"Shhh," Caitlin put her finger to her lips. "Not yet. We haven't made all our plans."

"Tell me what?" Roger asked eagerly.

"Oh, just a little idea we have for the council fund-raiser, but it's too soon to talk about it."

"Come on." Roger was becoming intrigued. "You're not being fair, Caitlin."

She paused. "Well, since you're our star soccer player, I can tell you it's going to be the hottest happening at Highgate this fall."

"Oh, yeah? What, a party?"

"No."

"A concert?"

She shook her head, her black-lashed, blue eyes twinkling. "I'm not going to stand here and play Twenty Questions with you, Roger. But when we decide to make our plans public, you'll be the first to know. I promise."

"Guess I'll have to settle for that."

"Anyway, Roger, I promise not to let any of this other stuff interfere with my supporting the team from now on."

At her look, Roger seemed ready to melt into his Nikes.

Just at that moment Jed Michaels stepped forward. It was a casual move on his part, as though he were just leaning in a little more closely to hear the conversation. His gaze rested on Caitlin.

Although she'd deliberately given the impression of being impervious to Jed, Caitlin was acutely aware of every move he made. She'd studied him enough from a distance to know that she liked what she saw.

Six feet tall, with broad shoulders and a trim body used to exercise, Jed Michaels was the type of boy made for a girl like Caitlin. He had wavy, light brown hair, ruggedly even features, and an endearing, crooked smile. Dressed casually in a striped cotton shirt, tight cords, and western boots, Jed didn't look like the typical preppy Highgate student, and Caitlin had the feeling it was a deliberate choice. He looked like his own person.

Caitlin had been impressed before, but now that she saw him close at hand, she felt electrified. For that brief instant when his incredible green eyes had looked directly into hers, she'd felt a tingle go up her spine.

Suddenly realizing the need for an introduction, Roger put his hand on Jed's shoulder. "By the way, do you girls know Jed Michaels? He just transferred here from Montana. We've already got him signed up for the soccer team."

Immediately the girls called out a chorus of enthusiastic greetings, which Jed acknowledged with a friendly smile and a nod of his head. "Nice to meet you." Dorothy's call had been the loudest, and Jed's gaze went toward the pretty blonde.

Dorothy smiled at him warmly, and Jed grinned back. But before another word could be spoken, Caitlin riveted Jed with her most magnetic look.

"I've seen you in the halls, Jed, and hoped you'd been made welcome." The intense fire of her deep blue eyes emphasized her words.

He looked from Dorothy to Caitlin. "Sure have."

"And how do you like Highgate?" Caitlin pressed on quickly, keeping the attention on herself.

"So far, so good." His voice was deep and soft and just slightly tinged with a western drawl.

"I'm glad." The enticing smile never left Caitlin's lips. "What school did you transfer from?"

"A small one back in Montana. You wouldn't have heard of it."

"Way out in cattle country?"

His eyes glimmered. "You've been to Montana?"

"Once. Years ago with my grandmother. It's really beautiful. All those mountains . . ."

"Yeah. Our ranch borders the Rockies."

"Ranch, huh? I'll bet you ride, then."

"Before I could walk."

"Then you'll have to try the riding here—eastern style. It's really fantastic! We're known for our hunt country in this part of Virginia."

"I'd like to try it."

"Come out with me sometime, and I'll show you the trails. I ride almost every afternoon." Caitlin drew her fingers through her long, black hair, pulling it away from her face in a way she knew was becoming, yet which seemed terribly innocent.

"Sounds like something I'd enjoy,"—Jed said, smiling—"once I get settled in."

"We're not going to give him much time for riding," Roger interrupted. "Not until after soccer season, anyway. The coach already has him singled out as first-string forward."

"We're glad you're on the team," Caitlin said. "With Roger as captain, we're going to have a great season." Caitlin glanced at Roger, who seemed flattered by her praise. Then through slightly lowered lashes, she looked directly back at Jed. "But I know it will be even better now."

Jed only smiled. "Hope I can live up to that."

Roger turned to Jed. "We've got to go."

"Fine." Jed nodded.

Caitlin noticed Dorothy, who had been silent during Jed and Caitlin's conversation. She was now staring at Jed wistfully as he and Roger headed toward the door.

Caitlin quickly leaned over to whisper, "Dorothy, did you notice the way Roger was looking at you?"

Her attention instantly diverted, Dorothy looked away from Jed to look at Caitlin. "Me?" She sounded surprised.

"Yeah. He really seems interested."

"Oh, I don't think so." Despite her attraction to Jed, Dorothy seemed flattered. "He's hardly ever looked at me before."

"You were standing behind me and probably couldn't notice, but take my word for it."

Dorothy glanced at the star soccer player's retreating back. Her expression was doubtful, but for the moment she'd forgotten her pursuit of Jed, and Caitlin took that opportunity to focus her own attention on the new boy from Montana. She knew she only had a moment more to make that unforgettable impression on him before the two boys were gone. Quickly she walked forward. Her voice was light but loud enough to carry to the girls behind her.

"We were just going in your direction, anyway," she called. "Why don't we walk along just to show you what strong supporters of the team we are?"

Looking surprised, Roger said, "That's fine by us. Right, Jed?"

"Whatever you say."

Caitlin thought he sounded pleased by the attention. Quickly, before the other girls joined them, she stepped between the two boys. Roger immediately tried to pull her hand close to his side. She wanted to swat him off, but instead, gave his hand a squeeze, then let go. She was pleased when Diana fell in step beside Roger. Turning to Jed, Caitlin smiled and said, "There must be a thousand questions you still have about the school and the area. Have you been to Virginia before?"

"A few times. I've seen a little of the countryside."

"And you like it?"

As they walked out the door of the building, Jed turned his head so that he could look down into her upturned face and nodded. There was a bright twinkle in his eyes.

Caitlin took that twinkle as encouragement, and her own eyes grew brighter. "So much goes on around here at this time of year. Has anyone told you about the fall dance this weekend?"

"I think Matt Jenks did. I'm rooming with him."

"It'll be great—a real good band," Caitlin cooed. In the background she heard the sound of the others' voices, but they didn't matter. Jed Michaels was listening to *her*.

They walked together for only another minute, down the brick footpath that connected the classroom buildings to the rest of the elegant campus. Caitlin told him all she could about the upcoming dance, stopping short of asking him to be her date. She wasn't going to throw herself at him. She wouldn't have to, anyway. She knew it would be only a matter of time before he would be hers.

It didn't take them long to reach the turnoff for the soccer field. "I guess this is where I get off," she said lightly. "See you around."

"See you soon," he answered and left.

Caitlin smiled to herself. This handsome boy from Montana wasn't going to be an easy mark, but this was an adequate beginning. She wanted him—and what Caitlin wanted, Caitlin got.

"You going back to the dorm, Caitlin?" Morgan asked.

"Yeah, I've got a ton of reading to do for English lit." Caitlin spoke easily, but her thoughts were on the smile Jed Michaels had given her just before he'd left.

"Somerson really piled it on tonight, didn't she?" Gloria Parks muttered.

"Who cares about homework," Caitlin replied. "I want to hear what you guys think of Jed."

"Not bad at all." Tenny giggled.

"We ought to be asking *you*, Caitlin," Morgan added. "You got all his attention."

Caitlin brought her thoughts back to the present and laughed. "Did I? I hadn't even noticed," she said coyly.

"At least Roger's got some competition now," Jessica Stark, a usually quiet redhead, remarked. "He was really getting *unbearable*."

"There's probably a lot more to Roger than meets the eye," Dorothy said in his defense.

"I agree. Roger's not bad. And what do you expect," Caitlin added, "when all he hears is how he's the school star."

The girls started crossing the lawns from the grouping of Highgate classroom buildings toward the dorms. The magnificent grounds of the exclusive boarding school were spread out around them. The ivy-covered walls of the original school building had changed little in the two hundred years since it had been constructed as the manor house for a prosperous plantation. A sweeping carpet of lawn had replaced the tilled fields of the past; and the smaller buildings had been converted into dormitories and staff quarters. The horse stable had been expanded, and several structures had been added—classroom buildings, a gymnasium complete with an indoor pool, tennis and racketball courts—but the architecture of the new buildings blended in well with that of the old.

"Caitlin, isn't that your grandmother's car in the visitors' parking lot?" Morgan pointed toward the graveled parking area off the oak-shaded main drive. A sleek, silver Mercedes sports coupe was gleaming in the sunlight there.

"So it is." Caitlin frowned momentarily. "Wonder what she's doing here? I must have left something at the house last time I was home for the weekend."

"My dream car!" Gloria exclaimed, holding one hand up to adjust her glasses. "I've told Daddy he absolutely *must* buy me one for my sixteenth birthday."

"And what did he say?" Jessica asked.

Gloria made a face. "That I had to settle for his three-year-old Datsun or get a bicycle."

"Beats walking," Morgan said, reaching into her bag for another candy bar.

"But I'm dying to have a car like your grandmother's."

"It's not bad." Caitlin glanced up at the car. "She has the Bentley, too, but this is the car she uses when she wants to drive herself instead of being chauffeured."

"Think she'll let you bring it here for your senior year?"

Caitlin shrugged and mimicked her grandmother's cultured tones. " 'It's not wise to spoil one.' Besides, I've always preferred Jaguars."

Caitlin paused on the brick path, and the other girls stopped beside her. "You know, I really should go say hello to my grandmother. She's probably waiting for me." She turned quickly to the others. "We've got to have a meeting for this fundraiser. How about tonight—my room, at seven?"

"Sure."

"Great."

"Darn, I've got to study for an exam tomorrow," Jessica grumbled, "but let me know what you decide."

"Me, too," Kim commented. "I was on the courts all afternoon yesterday practicing for Sunday's tennis tournament and really got behind with my studying."

"Okay, we'll fill you guys in, but make sure you come to the next meeting. And I don't want any excuses. If you miss the meeting, you're out!" Caitlin stressed firmly. "I'll catch the rest of you later, then."

All the girls walked away except Dorothy, who lingered behind. Just then, a tall, elegantly dressed, silver-haired woman walked briskly down the stairs from the administrative office in the main school building. She moved directly toward the Mercedes, quickly opened the driver's door, and slid in behind the wheel.

Caitlin's arm shot up in greeting, but Regina Ryan

never glanced her way. Instead, she started the engine and immediately swung out of the parking area and down the curving drive.

For an instant Caitlin stopped in her tracks. Then with a wide, carefree smile, she turned back to Dorothy and laughed. "I just remembered. She called last night and said she was dropping off my allowance money but would be in a hurry and couldn't stay. My memory really *is* bad. I'll run over and pick it up now."

As Caitlin turned, Dorothy lightly grabbed Caitlin's elbow and spoke softly. "I know you're in a hurry, but can I talk to you for a second, Caitlin? Did you mean what you said about Roger? Was he really looking at me?"

"I told you he was," Caitlin said impatiently, anxious to get Dorothy out of the picture. "Would I lie to you?"

"Oh, no. It's just that when I went over to talk to him, he didn't seem that interested. He was more interested in listening to what you and Jed were saying."

"Roger's just nosy."

"Well, I wondered. You know, I haven't had any dates since I transferred—"

"Dorothy! You're worried about dates? Are you crazy?" Caitlin grinned broadly. "And as far as Roger goes, wait and see. Believe me." She gave a breezy wave. "I've got to go."

"Yeah, okay. And, thanks, Caitlin."

"Anytime."

Without a backward glance, Caitlin walked quickly to the administration office. The story about her allowance had been a fabrication. Regina Ryan had given Caitlin more than enough spending money when she'd been home two weeks earlier, but it would be all over campus in a minute if the girls thought there was anything marring Caitlin's seemingly perfect life.

Running up the steps and across the main marble-floored lobby that had once been the elegant entrance hall of the plantation house, she walked quickly into the dean's office and smiled warmly at Mrs. Forbes, the dean's secretary.

"Hi, Mrs. Forbes."

"Hello, Caitlin. Can I help you?"

"I came to pick up the message my grandmother just left."

"Message?" Mrs. Forbes frowned.

"Yes." Caitlin continued to look cheerful. "I just saw her leaving and figured she was in a hurry and left a message for me here."

"No, she just met on some school board business briefly with Dean Fleming."

"She didn't leave anything for me?"

"I can check with the part-time girl if you like."

"Thanks." Caitlin's smile had faded, but she waited as Mrs. Forbes stepped into a small room at the rear.

She returned in a second, shaking her head. "Sorry, Caitlin."

Caitlin forced herself to smile. "No problem, Mrs. Forbes. It wasn't important, anyway. She'll probably be on the phone with me ten times tonight."

As Caitlin hurried from the main building and set out again toward the dorm, her beautiful face was grim. Why was she always trying to fool herself? She knew there was no chance her grandmother would call just to say hello. But nobody would ever know that: She would make certain of it. Not Mrs. Forbes, or any of the kids; not even her roommate, Ginny. Not anyone!

Like it so far? Want to read more? LOVING will be available in May 1985.* It will be on sale wherever Bantam paperbacks are sold. The other two books in the trilogy, LOVE DENIED and TRUE LOVE, will also be published in 1985.

*Outside the United States and Canada, books will be available approximately three months later. Check with your local bookseller for further details.

You'll fall in love with all the Sweet Dream romances. Reading these stories, you'll be reminded of yourself or of someone you know. There's Jennie, the *California Girl*, who becomes an outsider when her family moves to Texas. And Cindy, the *Little Sister*, who's afraid that Christine, the oldest in the family, will steal her new boyfriend. Don't miss any of the Sweet Dreams romances.

☐	24292	IT MUST BE MAGIC #26 Marian Woodruff	$2.25
☐	22681	TOO YOUNG FOR LOVE #27 Gailanne Maravel	$1.95
☐	23053	TRUSTING HEARTS #28 Jocelyn Saal	$1.95
☐	24312	NEVER LOVE A COWBOY #29 Jesse Dukore	$2.25
☐	24293	LITTLE WHITE LIES #30 Lois I. Fisher	$2.25
☐	23189	TOO CLOSE FOR COMFORT #31 Debra Spector	$1.95
☐	24837	DAY DREAMER #32 Janet Quin-Harkin	$2.25
☐	23283	DEAR AMANDA #33 Rosemary Vernon	$1.95
☐	23287	COUNTRY GIRL #34 Melinda Pollowitz	$1.95
☐	24336	FORBIDDEN LOVE #35 Marian Woodruff	$2.25
☐	24338	SUMMER DREAMS #36 Barbara Conklin	$2.25
☐	23340	PORTRAIT OF LOVE #37 Jeanette Noble	$1.95
☐	24331	RUNNING MATES #38 Jocelyn Saal	$2.25
☐	24340	FIRST LOVE #39 Debra Spector	$2.25
☐	24315	SECRETS #40 Anna Aaron	$2.25
☐	24838	THE TRUTH ABOUT ME AND BOBBY V. #41 Janetta Johns	$2.25
☐	23532	THE PERFECT MATCH #42 Marian Woodruff	$1.95
☐	23533	TENDER-LOVING-CARE #43 Anne Park	$1.95
☐	23534	LONG DISTANCE LOVE #44 Jesse Dukore	$1.95
☐	24341	DREAM PROM #45 Margaret Burman	$2.25
☐	23697	ON THIN ICE #46 Jocelyn Saal	$1.95
☐	23743	TE AMO MEANS I LOVE YOU #47 Deborah Kent	$1.95
☐	24688	SECRET ADMIRER #81 Debra Spector	$2.25
☐	24383	HEY, GOOD LOOKING #82 Jane Polcovar	$2.25

Prices and availability subject to change without notice.